MANIA

NOMAD SERIES — BOOK 5

K.A.FINN

Also by K. A. Finn

Nomad Series (Space Opera)

Ares

Nemesis

Perses

Chaos

Mania

Talon (TBA)

Broken Chords (Rockstar Romance)

Broken Rock

Fractured Rock

Split Rock (2023)

Crushed Rock (TBA)

Shattered Rock (TBA)

Blackjacks (Paranormal Romance)

Breaking Phoenix

Reviving Davyn

Defying Shep (TBA)

Unraveling Fallon (TBA)

A bit of a Nomad herself, **K.A. Finn** has
wandered around Ireland and the UK for decades
before settling back in Ireland with her husband and
kids (two and four legged).

Visit K.A. Finn online:

www.kafinn.com
(trailers, excerpts, artwork, playlists etc)

Facebook: kafinnauthor

Instagram: kafinnauthor

Twitter @K_A_Finn

Coming next

CRONUS

Nomad Series Book 6

Cover design by Deranged Doctor Design

Published by Cooper Publishing

www.cooperbookservices.com

Edited by Desert Mystic Literary Editing

www.desertmysticliteraryediting.com

ISBN: 978-1-914177-34-7

First Edition: January 2021

To Jenny. Thank you for being the most incredible friend I could ever have wished for xxx

MANIA

NOMAD SERIES – BOOK 5

K.A.FINN

PART 1

1 YEAR AFTER CHAOS

GRYFFIN – 29 YEARS OLD
BRAY – 24 YEARS OLD

1

Aleena's heart pounds in her ears in time to the intruder alarms. She loses her footing and slips on wet leaves. Ignoring the sting of grazed palms she pushes to her feet and increases her pace. She has to reach the town centre before their unwelcome visitors arrive.

She had been preparing dinner at home when the house shook, plates and ornaments jumping from the shelves. The immense battleship appeared out of nowhere, flying low over the village - no doubt in an act of intimidation. It was proving quite effective. As the hulking form settled into a nearby field, Aleena had sounded the alarm to disperse her people into the surrounding forest and the safety offered by the natural caves and mountains.

With no technology worth mentioning, Aleena had hoped Ultar would not attract the attention of raiding parties, and for years that was the case. She had not managed to gauge much about the vessel as it flew over her house apart from one thing as it moved away. On the back of the ship, a fierce bird-like creature glared down at her. That was enough for her to realise just how much trouble they were in. From the reports coming in from villages that have seen the ship, it is much worse than she could have ever expected.

Aleena has heard many tales from travellers about the uglier side of the Outer Sector, about groups who terrorise colonies without remorse. In all her years as leader of Ultar, she was fortunate not to have met any representatives of these groups. Until now.

It appears their luck has just run out. The Nomad ship, *Ares*, has arrived.

She doubts there is a colonist in the Sector who has not heard of the Nomad. Over the last year, under the leadership of her new captain, attacks by the flagship, *Ares*, had increased in frequency and devastation. The captain is well known for storming through village after village, taking whatever he wants and leaving blood and tears in his wake.

She had heard stories of the cruel and ruthless men that took what they wanted at the cost of hundreds of lives throughout the Sector. Knowing they are on her world sickens her, but she has no time to dwell on that.

She hurries to the centre of town, ushering anyone she passes to the safety of the forest. When she reaches the open square in the centre she knows she is too late. Dozens of masked men appear from the side streets, herding her people into the town hall. She takes a step back and bumps into someone behind her. She turns and gasps when she sees a broad man with a metal mask over his face. The purple lenses over his eyes seem to glow as he looks down at her. He lifts his gun and nudges her towards the rest of her people.

'I am the leader of this world. I want to speak to whoever is in charge.'

'No chance. Walk.' He lifts his weapon and nods towards the town hall. As much as she would like to argue her point, she knows it would fall on deaf ears. Her only option is to do as she is told... for now.

2

Gryffin steps off his transport and looks around the centre of the village. Ultar has been on his list for months, but this is the first time he's found himself in the area. The town is immaculate - much nicer than a lot of the places they find themselves. He subconsciously runs a hand over his uniform jacket. The leather is worn and badly cracked. His trousers have mud ingrained in the black fabric and if it rains, his boots will let the water in without a fight. All his men need new uniforms, but they barely have enough credits to cover food and repairs to the ship. Waterproof uniforms will have to wait.

His scuffed boots leave tracks in the carefully tended gravel path as he winds his way through the village. The houses surrounding the open area are well cared for with brightly coloured flowers and trees in the gardens or trailing up the front of the houses. The sound of farm animals carries from somewhere behind the buildings, but that's the only thing he hears. His men must have finished rounding up the Ultarans and securing them in the centre.

Each Nomad is wearing the same metal mask over their faces, but are easily identifiable by their tattoos. Only Gryffin himself has every inch of skin covered. The fact the captain of *Ares* is a cyborg is something he wants to keep on the down-low if he can. Rumours are rife but that doesn't mean he's going to add fuel to the fire by confirming it.

'Everyone secure?'

Sayber nods. 'They're a group of farmers - didn't put up much of a fight. Few casualties on their side. We've rounded up anyone we've found in the town hall.'

'Anyone you've found?'

'Seems they were expecting trouble at some stage. Most of the villagers scattered as soon as we broke orbit. We're looking but something is playing havoc with our scanners.'

'They have technology?'

Sayber shakes his head. 'Think it's natural. Sir, the leader wants to talk to you. I have been ignoring her demands but the damn woman won't shut up. Keeps going on about negotiating with you for the safe release of her people or something along those lines. You'd think the leaders would come up with something more original. It's the same script wherever we go.'

'Where is she?'

Sayber nods towards the largest building a few feet in front of them. 'Town hall with the others. You're not thinking of talking to her, are you?'

'Depends. Have you found any weapons?'

'None, sir. Seems they're hidden pretty well. Either that or they don't have any at all.'

'Keep looking. See if there's anything else we can use. I want us off the ground within the hour.' Sayber heads in the direction he came from while Gryffin moves towards the large wooden building at the top of the town square. He feels a little conspicuous walking along the perfectly tended path. His black uniform, weapons and metal mask are a harsh contrast to the flowers and greenery.

His men stand to attention as he nears the town hall. Six bodies lie in the centre of the square. He barely gives them a cursory glance. His men restrained themselves with only six casualties. He enters the town hall and faces a few dozen terrified, angry, and crying Ultarans.

A woman steps forward and stops in front of him. She's probably in her early forties – bit younger than most of the leaders he's dealt with. She's also better looking, with an athletic build and long blonde hair secured in a braid that reaches her waist. She crosses her arms and gives him an impressive glare. 'Are you the leader of this group of murderers?'

She's got guts too by the sounds of it. 'You the Ultaran leader?'

'I am.'

'Bring her.'

A few brave locals step forward to put themselves between Gryffin and the leader. He ignores the shouts of her protectors as he pulls out his gun. It takes two shots and two bodies for silence to be restored.

Gryffin steps over the fallen men and presses his gun to the leader's head. 'How many more do you want me to kill?'

'You did not need to take their lives.'

She swallows thickly as he applies a little more pressure, pushing the gun firmly against her forehead. 'How many more?'

'You have taken enough from us already. I do not wish to lose any more of my people.'

'Then you better tell them to stay the fuck back and do what they're told. Understood?'

She nods once. 'You have made your point.'

Gryffin holsters his gun and walks over to one of his crew. 'Is there an empty room?' He follows the man to a door at the left of the corridor and steps inside. The room is basic with a small window set high in the far wall, a large desk and three chairs.

'Bring her here.'

Gryffin sits on the edge of the table and massages

his arm. The injuries from Tyrat have healed but they took their time. The deep cut across his face has finally stopped its infernal itching. The scar is impressive. The thick pink line of new skin runs from his left cheek, across the top of his nose and ends above his right eye. The small consolation is that the guards hadn't taken his eye out with the broken bottle. The only thing still giving him issues is his arm. The pin Ryder fitted had done its job, adding strength to the limb as the bone knit together again, but it still aches when it's cold.

His newfound fame as a Tyrat escapee had more than helped them when they raided. Sayber had been right – the news spread faster than he thought possible. Within a few weeks, most colonies had heard about the new captain of the Nomad flagship. He wasn't complaining. Less resistance to landing parties meant less casualties – on both sides. He wasn't overly bothered about local fatalities, but he'd prefer to get in, take what they need, and leave without any problems. He thought Ultar would be the same. Eight bodies didn't worry him but he was expecting the Ultarans to keep the hell out of his way. Maybe a little chat with the leader would make sure they don't throw any more lives away.

3

Aleena takes a few deep breaths as she walks between four heavily armed men towards one of the offices off the main room. She is finding it difficult to get her thoughts in order. Those men were protecting her. That was their only crime - if you could even call it that. The leader had ended their lives as if he were extinguishing a candle. She doubts he gave it much more thought than that. What person could be so cold, so cruel, so unemotional to kill so easily? She does know one thing, however - negotiating with a person with such character traits would be an utter waste of her time. But it must be attempted.

This could be her one slim chance to bargain for the lives of her people. Either that or she is being taken to be killed. She chastises herself and pushes that thought away. It will not do her any good. She straightens her shoulders and tries to collect her thoughts. She did a quick headcount when she was brought to the town hall and more than half of her people have sought refuge in the woods. That does not mean they will not be found, but it gives her hope. Ultar does not have much to offer in payment, but she will give whatever is necessary to convince these men to leave without causing harm to anyone else.

Her thoughts are cut short as the men leading the party suddenly stop, sending her crashing into their backs. Neither man pays any attention as one opens the door and the other shoves her inside. She glares at the man who pushed her but he just closes the door in her face with an ominous thump. She looks to the front of the room and her breath catches in her throat.

Propped against the edge of the table, the Nomad leader appears so much more intimidating than he did with a gun in his hand. He clasps the edge of the table in his gloved hands as he looks towards the ground.

After a few moments of being completely ignored, Aleena finally finds her voice. 'My name is Aleena. I am the leader of Ultar. Would you care to give me your name?'

He does not reply. If not for his chest rising and falling she would have thought she was facing a statue. He does not even have the decency to look in her direction although with the mask covering his face it is difficult to be sure where he is looking. Aleena clears throat and tries again, this time with more confidence in her voice. 'I asked you a question.'

His head tilts slightly to the side. Instead of answering her question, he asks one of his own. 'Weapons. Where are they?'

Aleena frowns as she tries to understand what he is asking. 'What weapons?' He does not offer any clarification. 'Are you referring to our weapons?' Again, he does not say anything. 'We are a peaceful world. We do not need weapons... not until today it seems. You have taken eight lives for nothing.'

He shakes his head and rises from the table to an impressive height. Aleena stares up at him and forces herself to appear confident even though it is far from how she feels. 'I don't buy that.'

'I cannot help if you do not believe what I say. You asked me a question and I answered it truthfully. We do not have any weapons. We have nothing of value to you or your people.'

'I decide what's valuable, not you.' He crosses his arms and looks in her direction for the first time since she was pushed into the room.

Aleena's heart drops when she spots a patch of metal under the cuff of his jacket. The gravity of her predicament hits her as she examines him. A part of her hopes it is a weapon of some kind, but deep down she knows that is not the case. She has no doubt what she can see is a portion of his metal arm. Not only is the man in front of her the infamous captain of the Nomad flagship, but it appears rumours about him could be true. Until that moment, she had assumed any mention of metal limbs had been a result of far too much ale.

She licks her dry lips as she tries to keep in control of her emotions. 'You are the captain of *Ares*. I have heard stories about you and your ship.'

'Then why the hell are you arguing with me?'

'I am trying to explain our situation to you. We are a peaceful farming community who, until a few moments ago, has survived very happily without people such as yourselves coming to take what you believe you deserve.'

'People don't usually try to get on my wrong side. You're heading that way.'

She snorts. 'I fail to see how my situation could get any worse. You have landed on my world without permission. You have killed eight innocent Ultarans and taken my people captive. I presume you are raiding our food stores. No doubt our medical stores also. I do not see how questioning you at this stage can make things worse for us. You are here to do us harm. How many of us must die to give you what you want?'

'That depends on you.'

The rush of footsteps outside calls a stop to the conversation. A Nomad bursts through the door, panting slightly. 'Sir, a word in private.'

The captain and his man leave, closing the door behind them. Aleena waits for a second before she approaches the door. Just before she reaches out to try the handle, it bursts open, narrowly missing hitting her in the face. The captain stands in the doorway with a heavy gun in his hand. 'Is there anywhere you can hide your people?'

'Hide? You wish to hunt them down, is that it?'

'Slavers are coming. I'm pretty sure you don't want your people sold to fighting pits and rich men.'

'Slavers? They are real?'

'As real as I am.'

'How long until they reach Ultar?'

'*Ares* just picked them up on sensors. About ten minutes.' He speaks to a Nomad who comes up beside them. 'Pull three more teams off *Ares* then get her in the air.' He waits until the man has left before speaking to Aleena again. 'Are your people safe in the trees?'

'The trees?'

'We know they are hiding in the forest. Are they safe?'

Aleena opens her mouth to reply but stops herself in time.

The captain touches his ear. '*Ares*, visual of the Slaver's ship.' He holds a small screen out to Aleena and a heavy weight settles in her stomach when she sees a vessel on the screen. The familiar sight of their moon behind it all the evidence she needs.

'You are speaking the truth.'

'I don't lie. Slavers are coming for you and your people. Now, where are they hiding?'

'There are caves outside the village.'

He activates his comms unit. 'I need a transport to take the rest of the villagers to safety.' He listens then nods once before looking down at Aleena again. 'It's on the way. Bring everyone outside.'

'You are helping us?'

'I can't raid Ultar again if you're all dead or sold.'

Not quite the affirmation Aleena would have liked, but, if Slavers are here, the Nomad could be the lesser of two evils. 'Very well.'

ULTAR

The heat from the engines of the Slaver transport hits Aleena in the face as she watches it fly over the village. Thick black fumes billow out of the back, cloaking the village in a heavy cloud. She hurries to a group of villagers outside and ushers them into the Nomad transport. True to their word, the Nomad keep the Slavers occupied as the transport hatch closes and moves into the cover of the trees.

She rushes back inside and quickly checks each room to make sure everyone has been taken to safety. She finds three Nomad in the main room of the hall when she returns. The captain easily stands a head or more above the tallest in the group. He looks in her direction. 'Clear?'

Aleena nods once. 'I have checked. Everyone is gone.'

'Time to go then.' The two Nomad with him move towards the transport waiting outside. The captain pushes her inside as the other two Nomad take their positions in the cockpit. Her stomach lurches as the craft lifts off the ground and veers sharply to the left. She tightens the harness around her body and squeezes her eyes shut. Being in the craft is terrifying enough without dodging an enemy vessel. In any other situation she would laugh at her comment. The Nomad are hardly friends. In truth, she is escaping an enemy attack in an enemy vessel. If she survives it will be quite a miracle.

In the front of the ship, she can hear the captain shouting orders at the two men with him and presumably over his radio with other ships.

The captain storms through the ship, a heavy weapon in his hand. He opens the rear hatch and steps on the loading ramp as it lowers into thin air. Aleena can only watch in horror as he stands on the edge, his feet braced apart as he aims the gun above them. He follows the path of whatever he's tracking for a few seconds then fires once. Aleena screams as a transport falls from the sky, barely missing the Nomad still standing on the rear ramp as it crashes into the trees. The captain closes the hatch and returns to the front of the craft, completely ignoring Aleena.

A few seconds later the transport shudders and the captain returns. He pulls sharply on her harness. 'We're hit.'

'Hit? What do you mean?'

'We're crashing.' As he says the words, the vessel lurches down in a sickening motion.

Any response she may have tried to come up with flitters into nothing as the ship jolts again, its engines screaming as the pilot fights to keep it on course. Before she can stop him, the captain disappears into the cockpit as the ship impacts something and the lights go out.

ULTAR

Aleena groans as consciousness comes back to her. The first thing that hits her is the cold. She reaches out in the dark and pauses as her hand touches water. A heavy dread fills her. There is only one body of water large enough to accommodate the Nomad transport. They are in the lake. The suffocating panic threatens to consume her. There will be time for that once she has assessed her situation and figured out if it is truly hopeless as it seems.

Aleena removes the harness and tries to stand but a searing pain shoots up her leg. Something is wrong with it but in the darkness she has no idea how bad the injury is. The pain is intense so she remains still and takes a deep breath to steady her nerves.

'Hello?' Her voice betrays some of the panic she is trying to keep at bay. If she is the only survivor or the only one conscious, her odds of getting out of the transport are significantly reduced. 'Hello?'

Instead of a reply, she hears a groan and the sound of water being disturbed.

'Hello! Can you hear me?'

'Yeah.'

The smile cannot be restrained at the sound of the captain's voice. 'Are you injured?'

For a few minutes, all she can hear is someone moving in the water then the inside of the transport lights up. She shields her eyes as they adjust to the sudden brightness. When her eyes grow accustomed, she looks up and shrieks in surprise when she sees the robotic mask of the Nomad captain looming over her. 'You hurt?'

'Excuse me?'

'Are you hurt?' he asks again.

'My leg is injured. I cannot move it.'

He crouches down in the water and moves his hands along the floor of the transport. She feels his hand on her leg briefly then a searing pain travels up her leg. 'It's the support from the seat in front of you. It's gone through the back of your leg. I'll need to cut it to get you free.'

'Cut it? With what exactly? We are underwater and in case you had not noticed, the water is rising.'

He wades through the hold and disappears into the cockpit, completely ignoring her outburst. 'Captain!'

Time crawls for Aleena in the increasingly cold transport as she waits for him to bother answering her. He eventually reappears with a black box in his hands which he places on the seat beside her. He pulls out a device roughly two hands long and passes it to her. Before she can ask what it is, he opens a compartment over her head and hands her a lightweight, emergency blanket. 'Won't do much when the cabin fills, but it should help with the cold for now.'

'Thank you, Captain. Your men... are they-'

He shakes his head as he pulls more tools from the kit. 'Just us. My ship won't come back until the Slavers are gone. We're on our own till then.'

'But the craft is filling with water. How long must we wait?'

'As long as it takes. I'll cut the bar from the frame to release you. It'll hurt.'

For some reason, his blunt manner helps to calm her. 'It already hurts quite a lot.'

'It'll hurt more. Just stay still so I don't cut your leg.'

He sits on the floor next to her seat. By now, the water has risen to his shoulders. She watches in nervous silence as he attaches a small cylinder to one end of the tool and manoeuvres himself closer to her leg. 'Don't move.'

Before she can respond, he ducks under the water. A dull light emits from the end of the tool and the pain from the wound increases tenfold. Vibrations from the tool send the sickening sensation through the bar and up her leg. Aleena grips the edge of the seat and cries out in pain. A few minutes later, he comes up and wipes wet hair from his mask. 'You good?'

'Far from it, Captain, but I will be fine. How are you getting on?'

He climbs to his feet and rummages in the compartment above her head again, finally finding what he's looking for. He passes her a clear bottle of a pale green liquid. 'The crew picked this up from somewhere. It's alcohol. Might help with the pain.'

She is about to refuse then reconsiders as he ducks under again. Aleena removes the lid and, as he begins working again, takes a large mouthful. It tastes as unsightly as it looks but it does dull the pain a little. She clenches her jaw as the vibrations work through her leg again. The sensation turns her stomach adding nausea to the pain. Another shiver works through her body as the water reaches her waist.

He surfaces again, presumably to check on her then ducks under again. The next time he comes up, he drops the device on the seat next to her and kneels up. 'I'm going to move your leg away from the seat.'

She nods and sucks in a breath as he helps her lift her leg onto the bench beside her. Her stomach turns at the sight of the crude metal bar protruding from each side of her leg.

'I need to secure it, then I'm done.'

She nods, silently willing him to finish so he can get them out of here. The captain takes a bandage from the med kit and wraps it around the bar to ensure it will not move. He sits beside her and points to the bottle in her hand. 'That work?'

'It is without a doubt the worst thing I have ever tasted, but yes, it worked.' She looks across at him. 'I am quite... well, terrified. Do you honestly think we can survive this?

'The last few minutes will be tough. We have to wait for the cabin to fill. When that happens I'll open the emergency hatch and we can swim to the surface.'

'Ah.'

'Ah, what?'

'Perhaps this would be a good time to tell you I cannot swim.'

'I'll guide you. You won't be able to do much with your leg like that anyway.' He stands up and touches something behind his ear. With a gentle click, the mask retreats to expose a face that leaves her lost for words.

He is quite a bit younger than she imagined. She assumed he would be of similar age to her, but she would actually place him a decade or so younger - perhaps late twenties or early thirties. But it is not just his youth that surprises her. The Nomad leader is an incredibly attractive man. With his dark hair and deep blue eyes, he is striking. She frowns as something peculiar catches her attention. A ring of metal seems to be surrounding his eye, but his no-nonsense glare cuts off the question before she asks it.

'Move your hair aside.' A little confused, she does

as he tells her. The Nomad reaches across and holds the control behind her ear. With the slightest of pressure, it attaches to her skin. 'It has a small oxygen supply. It should last until we get to the surface.'

'But what about you?'

'I'll be fine.'

The silence stretches on as they wait for the ship to fill with freezing water. Aleena pulls the blanket around herself in a vain effort to keep the shakes away. Part is down to the cold and the pain but most is fear of their impending death. She is placing her life in the hands of someone she has no trust in. The water rises, along with her fear. Looking over at the Nomad, she can see nothing to suggest he is the least bit concerned about their predicament. His attention is firmly on the lever against the side wall. A lot is depending on that lever doing its job. If it does not release the back hatch, they will drown in this metal coffin.

'So, may I enquire as to why you are helping me?' Her teeth chatter loudly but she needs to talk. She needs to do something to take her mind off what is happening.

'I'm stuck in here too.'

She smiles. 'Very true. But you did not have to cut my leg free. Nor did you have to help us escape the Slavers. I am curious as to why. And do not reply with you cannot raid if we are all dead.'

He glances at her before focusing on the submerged handle.

'Are you going to ignore me?'

'What you said, it's the only reply.'

'You are an infuriating man, Captain. If your plan fails, we will be dead in a few minutes. Can you not just answer my question?'

'I hate Slavers. Hate everything about them.' He pulls his attention from the lever to look at her. His dark eyes appear to glow in the dim cabin, but perhaps that is her imagination. Or perhaps the alcohol. 'I will always kill a Slaver. No one should be property.' His eyes glow a little brighter then he turns away as he focuses on the handle again. A new chill settles over Aleena as she examines the man in front of her. He was speaking from experience. She thought Slavers and the Nomad were the ones to fear in the Sector. If someone owned the Nomad Captain at some stage, that group poses a significant threat to the Sector.

ULTAR

Gryffin wades back into the cockpit. The bodies of the two crew are in their seats, being held in place by their harnesses. After they get out of here in one piece, he'll use *Ares* to lift the transport out and give his men the send-off they deserve. Losing lives to scum like Slavers is a waste.

He tries the system again, but it's dead. Hitting the water after being hit by the Slavers had fried everything bar the emergency lighting. Gryffin looks out the front window into the gloomy lake. He estimates it'll take another ten minutes for the transport to fill. Only then will the pressure equalise and they'll be able to open the emergency hatch. If *Ares* isn't back by then he could be alone with a group of pissed off Ultarans. Not quite the way he planned for the day to end.

After relieving the fallen Nomad of their weapons, Gryffin opens his jacket and pulls his t-shirt up. A rough piece of metal torn from the console during the crash has done an impressive job on him. The wound isn't deep but it stretches from his side to his stomach. His clumsy first aid effort after the crash was failing miserably. Being submerged in freezing water probably wasn't helping either.

He wades into the hold. The Ultaran leader is propped up against the back of the craft wrapped tightly in the blanket. The freezing water and blood loss was hitting her hard. If she didn't get attention soon she might end up like the two in the cockpit.

He needs her alive. All this would be for nothing if the leader dies and they go away empty-handed. She holds the bottle out to him. 'Would you care for some?'

He shakes his head. 'It's disgusting.'

Aleena laughs. 'I cannot agree more. It has helped to put some warmth back in my limbs.'

Anything else she says is lost as the familiar spear of pain tears through his skull. Just what he needs right now. The badly timed power surge or malfunction hits again, driving the air from his lungs. Behind the pain, his thoughts become difficult to hold on to. He needs to get them out of here, but something else deep within needs more. It needs to be released, to fight, to do what it was programmed to do.

Just as Rayde wanted, the pain from his wound is calling to the implant, bringing it out whether he likes it or not. Years of training it to come out when he's in pain is going to backfire on him.

He drowns out the woman's incessant questions and, ignoring the buzz of the implant, focuses on the pain instead. He bites his bottom lip and presses his metal hand against the wound on his stomach. Through the fuzzy sensation in his brain, the pain registers, but not the way it did with Rayde. Instead of encouraging the implant to take control, it grounds him. He never fully felt in control of the implant. Using pain as the trigger to let it out worked, but it had nothing to do with him. Rayde would hurt him, the implant would take control and that would be it. He was just along for the ride. All he needed to do was not fight it.

This is entirely different. By using that same pain to push it down, he had gained a little of the control he's been lacking since Rayde found him. He could stop it. He can still feel it in the back of his head, but that didn't bother him. He'd won.

He lifts his head and frowns at the look on the woman's face. 'What?'

'Care to explain what you were doing?'

'Concentrating.'

'On what exactly?'

'Not killing you.'

'Excuse me?'

He shakes his head and thankfully, she doesn't push him on the issue.

'You know, you are not what I expected, Captain. How old are you?' She laughs and rests her head against the bulkhead. 'Apologies. I fear this green... stuff is going straight to my head. You are not going to tell me anything, are you?'

'No.'

She nods. 'As I expected... or should that be suspected?' She pauses then laughs. 'Either way, you are keeping up your mysterious stranger facade. I must applaud you for that.'

Gryffin reaches out for the bottle and she reluctantly hands it over. 'Think you've had enough.' He ducks under the surface and checks the emergency hatch again. When he resurfaces the water has reached the leader's chin, forcing her head up. She splutters as she tries to keep above the water.

Ignoring the screaming in his head at the contact, he lifts her onto the bench and stands in front of her so she can support herself against him. 'Thank you, Captain.'

'I'll put the mask on you now. Just breathe normally. The reserve tank should last until I get you to the surface.'

'Should?'

He activates the mask and she disappears under the surface. She grips his arms firmly in her hands but Gryffin breaks free. He presses his face against the roof of the transport and takes a few slow deep breaths to fill his lungs with the little air left. The implants supporting his lungs will keep oxygen in his system for a few minutes, but he's never tested them in a situation like this before. Not a hell of a lot he can do about that now.

As the cabin fills he swims to the bottom, ignoring the Ultaran leader as she desperately tries to grab on to him. The damn woman will use up her air supply if she keeps that up. He takes the lever in his metal hand, braces his boots against the floor and pulls.

Nothing happens.

He tries again and is rewarded with a little movement. Unfortunately, the lever bends in his grip instead of releasing. Gryffin closes his eyes, letting the implant have a little more control he tries again. At first it doesn't budge then little by little it gives in. The hatch drops - then stops. It's not wide enough for him to get out but the leader should be able to squeeze through. He reaches up and grabs her uninjured leg then pushes her out the gap. He'll find her and bring her to the surface if he gets out of here.

7

Ditching the rear ramp, Gryffin swims to the front of the ship and pushes past his two dead crew, held in place by their harnesses. He pulls his gun out and targets the window managing to crack but not break the glass. Looks like he's going to have to use brute force. He slams his metal fist against the crack finally breaking through. He pulls at the edges of the window to increase the size of the hole. A band tightens around his chest as he works. His implants are at their limit. If he doesn't get out of here he'll drown. With one last punch followed by a few kicks, he makes a large enough hole and pulls his body out.

Kicking hard, he rises through the lake and finally breaks the surface. He takes a few deeps breaths and looks around. No leader. Gryffin ducks back down and looks around. He finds her a few metres away, kicking frantically but going nowhere. She stops when she spots him coming towards her. Her hands grab at him and he resists the urge to push her off. He gets her to the surface and swims to the shore, dragging her after him.

Gryffin lowers the Ultaran leader on to the shore and turns her on her side as he removes his mask from over her face. She gasps and splutters a few times but seems to be in one piece. He pulls the control from behind her ear and attaches it to himself again. He wipes a hand over his face as he looks around. No sign of any Slaver ships but that means damn all. Once they smell new meat, they're nearly impossible to get rid of. Bodies mean credits. There's no way they'd leave without doing everything they could to make some profit - pay for the fuel and weapons they used at the very least.

'Thank you, Captain. I was sure you had left me.'

'We've got to move.' The Ultaran leader accepts his help to stand and looks up at him, a strange expression on her face. 'What?'

'Exactly how old are you?'

'I don't know.'

'How can you not know?'

'Can you walk?

'I will need support.'

Gryffin breaks a branch off the nearest tree and hands it to us to use as a crutch. 'Thank you. Have they left?'

He shakes his head. 'Doubt it.' He tries his radio. '*Ares*?' Still nothing but static. He needs to figure out how the hell Slavers block transmissions. The Nomad could put something like that to good use. 'We need to get you out of the open. They'll be looking for you.'

'Me? Why?'

'Leaders are worth more. Especially female ones. C'mon.'

He heads towards the relative safety of the trees. It takes a few seconds longer for the leader to hobble after him. After five minutes, he's ready to throw her back in the lake and go it alone. If the Slavers don't hear her crashing through the undergrowth he'd be bloody amazed. Might as well fire a flare into the sky and wait for them to come.

'You have to make that much noise?'

'Perhaps if you walked a little slower I could be a little quieter.'

'Perhaps I could shoot you and walk alone.'

Aleena pushes past him, keeping any comeback she wanted to say to herself. Gryffin glares at her back, using a fair amount of restraint to keep his gun from moving towards her. If he didn't need the damn woman alive he'd be sorely tempted. Once the Slavers are dealt with he needs to take what he can from this colony and get the hell out of here. If they break-even he'll be happy.

He scans the forest as he follows after Aleena. Something catches his eye to her right. Something mechanical. He races towards her, launching her into the undergrowth as the ground shifts, lifting into the trees sending leaves and other forest debris raining down on top of her. The heavy steel net swings from the trees a few steps from where she was seconds ago. Ideally, it would have been a few steps from where they both were but Gryffin seems to be all out of luck today.

He tests the steel netting, ignoring the leader's questions from the ground a good fifteen feet below him. Being trapped in the net is far from good but it does mean one thing. The Slavers want him or the leader, or both of them alive. That'll give him a chance to get close enough to make sure they regret that decision.

Using the holes in the net, he climbs higher and reaches out to test where the net is attached to the tree. It's steel too. If he had more room his metal arm could probably get through it. He climbs back to the bottom of the net, takes one of his guns from its holster and drops it through the net to the leader.

'What exactly do you expect me to do with that? Shoot you down?'

'They'll have heard the trap discharge. They'll come to check it out. Go to your people. Use that if you get into trouble. Just make sure you don't point it at my men. They'll kill you before you get close enough to explain.'

'I am not leaving you here.'

'I didn't get you out of the lake so they could capture you. My men didn't die so they could capture you. Take the gun and go to wherever your people are hiding.' He unties the pendant from around his neck and holds it through the net. 'Take this with you.'

She catches the pendent and examines the small griffin on the worn leather cord. 'I do not understand?'

'Safe passage with my men. Do not lose that.'

She ties it around her neck for safekeeping. 'You expect me to walk away and leave you like this?'

'You want to take on a team of Slavers and get me down, go for it.'

She looks down at the gun at her feet and hesitantly picks it up. 'What will you do?'

'They'll take me back to their ship. I'll try to get out before they leave the surface. Find someone on my crew. Tell them if I don't follow you after ten minutes, not to destroy the Slaver ship until they hear from me. Keep giving it hell, but keep it in the air. Now, go!'

Aleena nods and noisily clambers through the undergrowth.

Gryffin covers his face with his mask and settles in to meet the men who want to sell him. He pulls the makeshift bandage from his wound and presses his hand against it to force more blood out. He wipes the bandage across it to soak it in blood then ties it around his leg. Even from the ground, you'd easily notice the blood and assume he was badly injured. Which he is, but no one is going to see a wound under his t-shirt and jacket.

About half an hour passes before he hears a group moving in his direction. The Slavers approach their quarry, their posture relaxing when they notice he's injured and probably won't put up much of a fight. He smiles under his mask. It's always better when they underestimate him. They stand below him, each one with the same smug smile on their faces- similar to the one he has on his face.

'Not the leader but we'll get something for him.'

'There's always plenty of buyers for a Nomad. No shortage of enemies.'

'Yeah, but he's injured. Think he's dead?'

The man at the front gestures to his left. 'Get him down. No way to tell from down here.'

Gryffin remains as limp as possible as the net is lowered to the ground. The unlucky Slaver steps forward to untangle him as the others leave their guns trained on him. Gryffin waits until he is right in front of him before he clocks him in the face with his boot. The Slaver screams as his nose disintegrates into a bloody mess, removing him as a threat.

While still processing what just happened, Gryffin rolls to his feet and shoots the second guy between the eyes. His luck runs out with the third one. The Slaver gets his gun directed at Gryffin less than a second before he does.

'Drop it, Nomad.'

Gryffin does as he's told. He doesn't need a gun to end this.

'On your knees. Hands behind your head.'

Once Gryffin has obediently done as ordered, the leader relaxes. Not fully - just enough that Gryffin notices. 'We just want the leader. Where is she?'

'You miss the Nomad ship in orbit?'

'You miss my gun pointed at your head? Where's the leader?'

'Dead.'

The Slaver smiles. 'Hope not. If she is we'll have to take a hell of a lot of Nomad to make up for it.' He looks up as a transport appears above the trees and lands behind Gryffin. The six Slavers who emerge from the ship surround him, each one levelling their weapon at his head. 'Hang on one second.' He jams his gun against Gryffin's head, forcing it to the side. He rips the mask control from behind his ear and his smile grows when he sees the metal circling his eye. 'Well, well, well. If it ain't the captain himself. No need for the leader of Ultar when you got the Captain of *Ares*. Get the heavy restraints. Hear this one has a habit of escaping. Get everyone else secured. We'll head back to the ship again, unload, and come back for more.'

Any thoughts about fighting his way out fade as he hears those words. The bastards have already moved a load of prisoners back to their ship. As much as he wants to get out and save his ass, he can't leave anyone with the Slavers. Only one option - he's got to let them lock the restraints around his wrists and lead him back to their ship. The man who's done all the talking up to now shoves him into a cage at the back of the craft and seals the door.

'Let's go. Wouldn't want this one making a break for it.'

Gryffin steadies himself as the transport lifts off the ground and moves higher.

The leader leans against the side of Gryffin's cage and takes a swig from his flask. 'We may not have found the leader yet, but this trip is turning out more profitable than I thought.' He raises his flask to the six Ultarans chained to the railing running along the side of the craft. 'But you... well, you're the big score for us.' He takes another swig from his flask and walks back to the cockpit. Gryffin looks over at the Ultarans. They're looking at him like they're not sure who they should be more wary of - him or the Slavers.

Gryffin ignores the Ultarans as he discretely tests his chains. There's a chance he can break them but he will have to use the implant. He'll wait until they get back to the ship. No telling how many Nomad they've bagged.

Kellyn steps out of the cave as someone approaches. From what he can hear, they've been injured. He lifts his gun and crouches down behind the bush. The Ultaran leader stumbles out of the undergrowth looking like she's been through hell and back. He rushes over to her, raising his weapon when he notices the gun in her hand - Gryffin's gun. 'Where's the captain?'

She points behind her as she catches her breath. 'In a Slaver trap. A net of some sort. It is suspended from the trees.'

'You're going to tell us where.'

She shakes her head. 'I fear it is too late. I passed a group of Slavers moving in that direction. They would have reached him by now.'

Kellyn curses and gestures to the weapon in her hand. 'Drop that and get into the cave.'

She drops the gun and slowly raises her hand to her neck. She pulls down the collar and lifts the pendant out. 'How the hell did you get that?'

'Your captain gave it to me to prove what I am about to say came from him and him alone.' She unties it from around her neck and holds it out to him.

'Best you hang on to that. He gave it to you, not me. Bit of advice though - you lose that and he'll kill you.'

She fixes it around her neck again, securing it with a double knot to be sure.

'So, what's the message?'

'He said that if he does not follow me after ten minutes, not to destroy the Slaver's ship until you hear from him. You must... 'give it hell, but keep it in the air'. I presume that makes sense to you.'

'Yeah. The giving it hell part won't be a problem. With comms down, it'll be fucking impossible to tell *Ares* to lay off. The problem is, there's every chance she'll bring the ship down with the captain on board. Not much we can do about it. C'mon, let's get you inside.'

He slips his arm around her waist and helps her into the cavern. She lowers to the ground and thanks a woman as she hurries over to see to her injury. 'Did everyone reach safety?'

Kellyn shakes his head. 'Got most of you out but from what I've been told, there's about half a dozen, maybe more, missing.'

'So they have some of my people and your captain. Is there anything that can be done to help them?'

Kellyn shakes his head. 'No need. The captain will sort it out.'

'I do not know if you heard me correctly. The Slavers have him. He is their prisoner.'

Kellyn rests his gun on his shoulder as he smiles down at her. 'Not so sure that's the way it went. If I know the captain, instead of getting him, he got them. They just don't know it yet.'

'But he is just one man on a ship of many Slavers.'

'Hardly seems fair on them, does it?'

SLAVER SHIP

Gryffin obediently follows the rest of the prisoners to the cells on the Slaver ship. As well as the ones on the transport with him, another twelve Ultarans occupy the line of cells in the cargo hold. No Nomad that he can see. He doubts they'd be held somewhere else so can assume he's the only one they got. That's good. Everyone being held in the same place will make things easier.

He plays the dutiful prisoner as he is stripped of his jacket and gloves. The leader whistles as he takes in the implants. 'Well, well, well. Now we know why there's so much interest in you.'

His men reattach the restraints and fix them to a ring embedded in the ceiling of the cell. 'Fit a second set of restraints. Can't be too careful.' With the second set locked in place, they lift him off the ground by his arms, suspending him a few feet from the ground. 'Back to the surface. See who else you can pick up.'

Gryffin smirks as the ship rocks. *Ares* isn't holding back. 'You pissed someone off?'

The Slaver snorts. 'May have a different outlook if they knew I've got you.'

'They know. Won't make a difference.'

'Is that so. Well, best we get the hell out of here then. Was going to head back for more but you'll make up for that.' He takes a step back and examines Gryffin. Trying to work out how many credits he can get no doubt. 'I reckon with a bit of strict retraining, someone will pay a hefty sum for you. Even with the scars and all that shit attached to you, you'll turn a few heads. Might get you a female owner. Someone to keep entertained. How's that sound?'

'Don't think I'll make a good pet.'

The Slaver makes a face. 'Perhaps. Could be fun giving it a shot though. Hang tight. We'll be on our way soon enough.'

He locks the cell behind him, still laughing at his 'hang tight' joke as he walks away.

Gryffin's going to enjoy killing him. First things first – get out of the cell. He examines his bonds and smiles. The restraints may have to stay on but he's sure he'll be able to break the chains linking them. He grabs on to the chains with both hands and lifts his feet up and over his head. Hanging upside down, he puts his feet to either side of the ring in the ceiling. After firming his grip on the chains attached to his wrists, he braces and pulls. Nothing happens for a few seconds then with a groan, the ring comes loose from the ceiling. Gryffin twists, landing on his feet, catching the ring before it hits the ground and brings guards running.

He stands on the chain linking his wrists and yanks his mechanical arm back. The chain snaps under the pressure. He places the ring on the ground and examines the cell door. The locks don't put up much of a fight when faced with his fist. The Ultarans in the surrounding cells have climbed to their feet by the time he gets out.

'Hey! What about us?'

'Stay here and shut up,' Gryffin mutters as he walks away

He closes the door to the cells, muting the whining from the Ultarans. The guard at the end of the corridor goes down quickly and Gryffin relieves him of his weapon. He checks the ammunition. Should be enough to get him to the command deck.

He peers around the corner to find two Slavers talking to each other. The body of the first hasn't hit the ground before his mate falls beside him. Gryffin helps himself to their weapons then steps over them. It's a better end than they deserved.

Gun raised, he climbs the stairs to the next deck and

slows as the mutter of voices echoes down the corridor. A lot of voices. Must be the command deck. He flattens himself against the wall and checks around the corner. Jackpot.

From his position, he can see five men. He steps out from around the corner and fires again and again as he strides towards the command deck. The five men are dead before anyone moves to defend themselves. As he gets closer, he sees more crew at various stations around the deck. The element of surprise works in his favour as three more fall. One lucky Slaver gets a few shots off, but at that stage, he's already on the command deck. He ducks behind a station, crouching over the body of a fallen Slaver as he bides his time. The Slaver fires and Gryffin follows almost immediately with one of his own. A shout signals he's hit home. Without waiting to check, he leaves cover, keeping low as he crosses the back of the room. He dives behind another console as he fires, taking down the last upright man he can see.

Gryffin walks over to the captain. Blood flows freely from a hole in the side of his neck, soaking his shirt and chair. He fires again. The round enters the captain's forehead, goes through the back of the chair and embeds itself in the unit behind him.

As Gryffin stares down at the man, his face changes for an instant. The Scientist lies in the captains' place, the blood from the bullet wounds staining his filthy lab coat. He clenches his fists around the gun as more details come into focus, bringing the Scientist out of the darkest corners of his mind. Being on this ship is fucking with his head. He looks down at the restraint locked around his arm. Had the Slavers bought him from his parents then sold him to the Scientist? It's possible. Anything is possible if he thought about it enough. He could invent all kinds of reasons he was on the station. Until he finds who did this to him he'll never know why.

Gryffin stares at the image his messed up brain created and lifts his gun. By the time his gun is empty, there's nothing left of the Scientist's face. Or the Slaver captain.

ARES

Gryffin storms past the Nomad at the airlock and climbs the stairs to the command deck. Sayber laughs as Gryffin lowers into the seat. 'Hell of a way to get back to *Ares*, sir.'

'Launch the tethers. Bring the ship back to Ultar with us. They've got Ultarans in the cells.'

'You heard the captain. You good, sir?'

'What?'

'Are you okay, sir. Look like you've seen a ghost.'

The image of the ruined face of the Scientist flashes into his mind. He pushes his hand against the wound on his stomach and the pain quenches the memory. If hurting himself keeps the implant at bay along with the memories, he'll keep it up. Having control over something means more than a little pain.

'Sir? You okay?'

'Yeah. Comms back yet?'

'Nope. Once we get things sorted on the surface we can tear the ship apart. Whatever they're using to block comms should be there... somewhere.' Sayber frowns and turns to face Gryffin. 'Seems you're leaking, sir.'

Gryffin glances down at his stomach and the blood trailing down the front of his trousers. 'Cut from the shuttle crash. It's fine.'

Sayber nods. 'Of course it is.' He gestures behind him and a med kit is handed to him. 'Lift your top.' Sayber sucks in a breath as he examines the wound. 'It'll need stitches but you should live. I'll get Ryder set up in the med bay.'

'No. Fix it here.'

Sayber raises his eyebrows but doesn't argue. 'Top off and stand up so I can see it better.'

He works on the wound while Gryffin stares out at Ultar. 'You think they have weapons?'

Sayber glances up from the wound. 'Ultar?'

'Yeah.'

'You've been on the surface more than me. Can't say for sure.'

'They would have used the weapons against us if they had them. Definitely against the Slavers. If we weren't here they'd be in cages. I don't think the colony has any fucking weapons.'

'That would be a first, sir.'

'Ultar is going to end up costing us more than we'll make.'

'Got the Slaver ship to salvage. Bound to be something onboard we can sell. Must be food and medical supplies down there we can take. Won't be a total bust.'

'You stay here when we land. Get the ship repaired as much as you can. Stick to vital systems. The rest we can deal with later. Get another team over to the Slaver ship. Tear the thing apart. I want the tech they use to block transmissions. Once we're done, take it off the surface and destroy it.

'Yes, sir.' Sayber fixes a bandage over the wound and gets to his feet. 'All done.' He picks up the blood-soaked, wet t-shirt and grimaces. He points to the first Nomad he sees and hands it to him. 'Get the captain something a little less damp to wear.'

Gryffin sits back on his chair as *Ares* touches down in a field outside the village. He takes the clean t-shirt from the Nomad and pulls it on. The wound feels so much worse with the stitches in it. At least he won't be leaving a trail of blood behind him. He opens the compartment on the side of his seat and takes his spare gun out. They may have taken care of all the Slavers on the main ship but that still leaves a few on the surface. Time to go hunting.

11

With help from two of her people, Aleena follows the Nomad teams back towards the village. All she had been told was that the Slavers were no longer a problem. As to exactly what that means, she has no idea. All she is concerned about is finding out how many of her people had been taken. Losing even one of them to a group of Slavers is more than she can bear.

She enters the town square and stops as she stares at the sight in front of her. Nomad are dragging bodies into the square and depositing them in the back of a transport. 'What is all this?'

Kellyn gestures for her to follow him. 'We took back

control of the colony. All Slavers are dead.'

'Dead? How many of my people were taken to the main ship?'

Kellyn smiles and nods to the far side of the town. Another group of Ultarans are making their way into town from the fields outside the village. She fails to understand what happened until she spots the tall Nomad at the far side of the group. The Nomad Captain.

'I thought he was captured.'

'Like I said - he got them not the other way around. He got out of his cell and took the ship.'

Aleena limps over to the Nomad captain. 'I am surprised to see you again.'

'Get your people into the town hall. Keep everyone there while we make sure we've rounded up all Ultarans and Slavers.'

'For how long? I am sure people would like to return to their homes.'

He storms away from her without responding. She follows Kellyn into the hall to see more of her people being ushered inside under armed guard. The Nomad may have taken care of the Slavers, but that has only put the Ultarans back under Nomad control.

'I need to speak to your captain.'

Kellyn shakes his head. 'Not happening. We've given your doctor a med kit. He's in one of the spare offices. Get that leg seen to. We'll get some food and water brought in.'

'I do not understand. You helped us. Why keep us

here like this?'

'We took down the Slaver ship because it was a Slaver ship. Whether it helped the colony or not wasn't a reason. See to your people.' He walks to the door of the hall and joins the other equally heavily armed Nomad blocking the exit.

12

Gryffin swings his legs out of his bed and slowly makes his way over to the door. He leans heavily against the wall and hits the controls. 'What is it, Sayber?'

'Got the woman from the village. Wants to talk to you. Pretty damn insistent. Tried everything except shooting her. Willing to do just that if you give me the go ahead.'

If he hadn't gone to so much trouble to keep her alive he might have been tempted. 'Bring her to the training room. I'll talk to her there.'

Sayber frowns. 'You want her on board? A woman?

But, sir, we've never had a woman on board.'

'I'm too damn tired and sore to worry about that right now. Just bring her in.'

'But what if she tries to-'

'What? Kill me? We've already figured out they don't have weapons. I can survive anything else she throws at me. Just do it.'

Sayber leaves, bringing the other numerous objections along with him. Gryffin doesn't know where the tradition or superstition about women on the ships came from and he couldn't care less. The Ultaran leader isn't a threat to him or his ship.

He looks over at his bed and the t-shirt lying at the end of it. It's ridiculous, but the idea of having to take the few steps to retrieve it seem a few steps too far. He's barely had an hours sleep in the last few days and his body is kicking his ass because of it. The last thing he wants to do is meet with Aleena but he needs to leave Ultar with something. If he has to lock her in a cell while his men tear the village apart so be it.

He summons the energy to grab his t-shirt from the bed and slowly pulls it over his head, careful to keep it off the bandage on his stomach. He makes his way to the training room trying to not let on how tired he is.

From the second they landed on this damn planet they've gone from one crap situation to the next. Even if they find a chest of credits, it's not going to make up for the effort they've put into the last few hours. The damn place must be cursed. He'll meet with the leader. Finish with the Slaver ship. Pull the transport from the lake. Take whatever they can find worth anything from the town and get the hell off this world. He never wants to set foot on Ultar again.

13

Aleena waits at the bottom of the ramp under the watchful eye of three Nomad guards. Each of them has their weapon directed at her, which is a little unnecessary considering she is armed with nothing more than her bare hands. She has been waiting in the cold for close to ten minutes and will continue to wait until the Nomad leader agrees to see her. Her first few requests had resulted in laughter and a refusal to even announce her presence. It took repeated requests to be taken seriously.

To her amazement, the Nomad had released her people from the town hall a few hours ago. There had been no explanation from the leader. As there had also been no attempt to leave the surface, their fate is still very much in the hands of the Nomad. Hence her visit to the ship. They may have said her request would be passed to the captain but that did not mean he would accommodate her. One thing she had gleamed since first meeting the man is that he is nothing if not unpredictable.

An unmasked, tall, dark-haired man with a long ponytail and a goatee approaches her from inside the ship. He looks at her suspiciously for a few seconds before he speaks. 'I'm Sayber, second in command of *Ares*.'

'I would usually reply with how much of a pleasure it is to meet you, but I think in this instance I will refrain. You have left your face uncovered.'

'You've already seen the face we're trying to hide.' He smiles briefly. 'Why do you want to see the captain?'

'I have something to discuss with him.'

'What?'

'I am the leader of this colony. I would like to speak to the leader of your ship. Surely that is not too difficult to comprehend.'

Sayber crosses his arms and Aleena fears she may have pushed too hard. She needs to see the captain, but that task will prove impossible if she cannot get past his crew. She is about to back step a little when he drops his arms and moves to the side. 'He'll give you a few minutes. C'mon.'

Aleena follows him into the large cargo hold, past land and air transports and up to the next level. She ducks under the hatch and along cramped, dimly lit corridors. Aleena stares around her in amazement.

Many transports had visited her colony over the years, but never anything of such size. *Ares* is impressive, if a little unloved. She may not know a lot about vessels but she does know that a great deal of her internal metalwork has been removed, exposing her inner workings. Most of the Nomad she's seen so far are similarly unkempt. Even the second in command appears to have patches on his uniform. She watches a group of Nomad who fall silent as she passes. Their pale, gaunt faces follow her until she rounds the corner.

The realisation of their situation hits her. The crew is starving. They may act as a formidable group but they are also in trouble if she is reading the signs correctly. They were in the process of clearing the food and medical stores on Ultar. She never thought about the reason for their actions. Now that she sees the crew and ship she is convinced they attacked out of necessity. She hides the smile from her face. This information can only work in her favour.

Another Nomad stares strangely at her as she pushes past in the cramped corridor. Once out of earshot she taps Sayber on the shoulder. 'Why are the crew looking at me strangely?'

'You're the first woman who's stepped foot on *Ares*.'

'Surely you do not mean ever?'

'Nomad ships don't allow women on board. Bad luck.'

'I would imagine that would cause issues with finding and keeping a partner.'

He glances over his shoulder at her. 'We're about the survival of the group, not socialising.'

'Forgive me, but unless Nomad are drastically different physically, woman are necessary for the survival of a species.'

Sayber stops at a large double door and leans against the wall. 'You're not born a Nomad - you're initiated.'

She shrugs. 'If you ask me it sounds like a very lonely existence.'

'I didn't ask you. You shouldn't even be here, lady. You're a security risk and I take those damn seriously. Am I making myself clear?'

She nods and clasps her hands together to keep them steady. He has mirrored her thoughts - she should not be here, but her people need her to find a way out of this. 'I assure you, I will leave your ship as soon as I possibly can. After I speak to your captain.'

'I don't know what you're hoping to achieve by talking to him. He may have saved your life on the transport but that doesn't mean he's going to shake your hand and leave the colony. You're not kindred spirits or anything like that. If you're thinking you can somehow get in touch with his softer side you're wasting your time... and his. It doesn't exist.' He steps closer to her and lowers his voice. 'You know I said we're not born Nomad? Well, he's as close to a born and bred Nomad as you get. His sole purpose is the survival of the Nomad. You should remember that.' He opens the door and gestures for her to enter. 'Good luck.' His smile has little warmth in it as he turns away and shuts the door behind him.

Aleena swallows and forces her hands to unclench. Being on this ship, among these people, is as far from her comfort zone as anything can be. She wants nothing more than to leave here and go back to her house, sit on the couch by the fire, and forget this nightmare ever happened. But she does not have that luxury. Despite what the Nomad just said, she believes there is negotiation room with the leader. What had he said in the transport? They cannot come back and raid again if everyone is dead. It is hardly a comforting thought but it gives her a small sliver of hope something can be done.

She straightens her shoulders and slowly approaches the top of the metal stairs leading to the vast room below. She stops at the top and peers over the edge. The room is an impressive size, stretching into the darkness in front of her. Machinery that has seen many better days lines each side of the space. She recognises exercise equipment among the scrap, some still in use but most so badly damaged it is beyond repair. Large dents decorate a lot of the wall still visible in the gloom. She realises with a sinking feeling that the dents are fist size. They must be from the metal hand of the leader.

Aleena looks over her shoulder at the door and resists the intense pull back to safety. Movement below her catches her attention so she creeps forward. The captain is below her, just out of the shadow of the balcony. His metal hand is braced against the wall as he leans forward with his head down.

Some of the fear dissipates as she watches him push away from the wall and lower on to the bench. He massages his flesh arm in his metal one. He closes his eyes and rests his head against the wall as he takes a shaky breath. He may be a born and bred Nomad, but he's still a human. Under the machinery and the threats, he's a young man who's injured and in obvious pain. If he carries on with his chosen path in life, she fears there will be a lot more pain in his future.

She cannot imagine a happy ending for him or any of the Nomad. Moving from colony to colony, fighting for survival, suffering injury for something as basic as food and medical supplies. She cannot help but wonder how much better a life they could have if they gave up their ships and settled on a colony.

She smiles at the idea of him working in a field, harvesting crops. She fails to think of anywhere he would seem at home - except perhaps for this ship. Whatever his reasons for getting the various modifications, she knows it was not for the benefit of farming. Perhaps he ruled out a life such as that years ago? She fails to see how someone so young could have made such a drastic decision about their future.

He looks up at her and she freezes as his dark blue

eyes meet hers. Whatever reasons he may have had for making the modifications she knows one thing - they certainly help to turn the attractive young man into an intimidating leader for the Nomad.

14

Gryffin sits up as the Ultaran leader slowly makes her way down the stairs to the training room. His arm hurts like hell and the wound on his stomach is throbbing but she's not going to know that. If the Nomad are going to get anything from the colony she needs to know they're still a serious threat. He stares at her as she makes her way across the room, leaning heavily on her crutch. She stops in front of him and clasps her hands together 'How are you feeling, Captain?'

'My men said you won't go until you talk to me. So talk.'

She gestures to the bench beside him. 'May I?' He nods once, just wanting to get this chat over with as soon as possible. 'I believe I am the first female to board your ship.'

He doesn't respond.

'Are you going to speak to me or is this going to be a one-sided conversation?'

'You wanted to talk to me - not the other way round.'

'Very well. As the appointed leader of Ultar, I wish to clarify what happens now. Before the Slavers so rudely interrupted, you were in the middle of telling me what you were going to take from Ultar by force.'

He rubs his forehead and takes a deep breath. 'And you want me to reconsider, right?'

She smiles at him. 'That would be greatly appreciated.'

'No.'

She stares at him. 'No? Do you expect me to accept that and let you raid our colony?'

'We have control of your people.'

'So you destroy our home and leave. Then what? Do you move to the next and do the same again, and again. Is that how you plan to spend the rest of your lives? Surely there has to be a better way than just stealing enough to keep you alive until the next colony?'

Gryffin pushes to his feet and moves towards the stairs. 'We'll leave enough supplies to last you a few days. Don't get in our way.'

'Then you sentence us to death, Captain.' She hurries after him as fast as her injured leg will allow. 'Why fight the Slavers, why save my life if you are going to kill us anyway?'

'I wasn't saving your life. I stopped the Slavers from refilling their cages. Now, I can either leave you alive and take the supplies or put a bullet in each of you and take the supplies. I couldn't care less which one you pick.'

Her face drops at his words, but he doesn't back down. It's the truth. If the Slavers hadn't fucked things up they'd already be off the planet and far away from this situation.

'What if there is another option?' she says after a long pause.

'There isn't.'

'Sit down.'

Gryffin frowns at the woman. 'What?'

'I said sit, Captain. Please.' He looks over at the bench and back to the woman. Despite everything, he can't help but be impressed by her stubbornness. 'Sit before we both fall. I do not know about you but after the day I had yesterday I could do with sitting down. I promise I will not take up much more of your time.'

To stop himself from falling as she irritatingly noticed, he makes his way back over to the bench and lowers on to it.

She sits beside him and stretches her injured leg out in front of her. 'I have been giving this much thought since our... forced confinement yesterday. As much as I am loathed to admit, I am somewhat grateful to you and your men. Your feelings towards the Slavers is more than justified. Your actions yesterday saved my people. You and your Nomad appear to be the lesser of two evils.'

He raises his eyebrow, wishing she'd get on with it and let him get back to bed.

'Would you consider trading.'

'What?'

'Ultar is reasonably self-sufficient, but that does not mean we have everything we would like to have. What we lack is the means to physically search for and retrieve these items.'

'You want a transport?'

Aleena laughs and shakes her head. 'Good gracious no. My people prefer to keep our feet firmly on the ground and we do not plan on changing that. No, what I suggest is that we strike up an agreement. We will give your crew food and medical supplies and you agree to trade something with us in return - as well as leaving us alive of course.'

'Like what?'

Aleena shrugs as she looks around the training room. She straightens when she sees the pile of metal scrap in the corner. 'Metal - tools mainly. Things to help us work the land, mend houses. No weapons, however. Even after recent events, I would prefer to keep Ultar away from that path if at all possible. You could also assist with the repairs to the village.'

'So you want me to trade the little we have for what

we want instead of just taking it at no cost to ourselves.'

'I would not put it quite like that. It is like you said in the transport. You cannot steal from us if we are dead. I am merely offering a solution based on your own words. Trade and keep coming back. A mutually profitable solution.'

Gryffin slowly leans against the wall, resisting the urge to rub his arm. All the exertion over the last few hours isn't agreeing with it. 'You'll need to arm yourselves at some stage.'

'I am aware of that, Captain. That leads me to the second part of my proposal. Would you consider offering Ultar your protection? I am not suggesting that you stay here - far from it. More so that you make it known you are keeping an eye on the settlement - for a fee of course.'

Gryffin stares at the woman in silence as he processes everything she said. What she is offering is far removed from anything he's ever done. He's not aware of any Nomad ship that operates in a protection capacity. As far as he knows, it's never been done before.

His first instinct is to contact Rayde and discuss it with him, but he quickly dismisses it. *Ares* is his ship and he is her captain. If he can't make a decision like this without help from Rayde, he has no right to sit in her command chair.

'I understand this is a far cry from your usual day-to-day operation,' she says as if reading his mind, 'but

I believe it will benefit both parties. Your crew is clearly in need of food. When was the last time any of you had a good decent meal? Agree to this and we will supply you with a plentiful supply of food immediately.'

Gryffin doesn't respond, letting the silence stretch on for an uncomfortable few moments. His crew is hungry - she's right about that. The Nomad way of life assured they are a group not to be messed with, but that reputation means damn all if they can't stand on their own two feet thanks to empty stomachs. 'You want us to have dinner with you as if we're friends?'

'Friends may be a stretch. I am simply trying to find the best solution for both parties. We will not survive if you take all our food and medicines. We need it. However, I can see that your crew are also in desperate need of food and medical supplies. So we agree to work together. That is my solution. Do we have an agreement or not?'

'Nomad don't deal.'

'Surely it is better to have a partner you can deal with than a colony you destroy and cannot go back to? Also, if we traded, you and your men would be most welcome to take a few days leave on the surface... occasionally. It is a winning situation for both our people, Captain.'

'We couldn't always come if you're attacked. We move around a lot.'

'I understand that. I believe merely letting would-be attackers know they would face the Nomad if they step out of line would be a valuable deterrent.'

He readjusts his position again to relieve pressure from his wound. The woman makes a good case and he's sorely tempted. He knows the men would appreciate somewhere safe to spend a few days off the ship. *Ares* is their home but even the more dedicated crew needs fresh air every now and again. The food and extra credits would be welcome too. There's not much left of the ship they can strip and sell. The more he thinks about it, the more sure he is that this is a good idea. The problem is, as soon as he makes the deal he'll change the path of *Ares* forever. The group could certainly do with the credits and if this works with Ultar, other ships could do the same. It could be a new era for the Nomad.

If the protection side of the deal is going to work, the reputation of the Nomad would have to be solid. At their core, the Nomad are fighters. Gryffin has no intention of changing that, but maybe he could turn them from petty raiders to profitable mercenaries. They could still fight but get paid for it. Better that than thieves with barely enough credits to keep their ships going. Rayde would have something to say about it, but Gryffin knows this is the right thing to do. The Nomad should be respected and feared for the right reasons. Taking from helpless villagers isn't the way to do that.

'Fine.'

Aleena blinks a few times and frowns. 'Excuse me?'

'I said fine. We'll deal.'

15

Gryffin steps off *Ares'* loading ramp and takes a deep breath. Even from this distance, he can smell food and hear laughter from the town centre. After he agreed to trade, Aleena had quickly arranged a dinner for that evening. Gryffin had checked the area before letting his crew loose. From what he could see, Aleena and her people hadn't held back. Seven large tables had been set up in the centre, each one laden with loaves of bread, fruits and meat. His stomach growled loudly as the smell had hit him, but he ignored it and went back to the ship. He didn't want to leave her unguarded, but also didn't want to deny any of his men the chance to have a decent meal. He looks at the dried ration bar in his hand and grimaces.

'I do not blame you. It does not look very appetising.'

Gryffin relaxes when he spots Aleena and an Ultaran man at the side of the ramp. 'What do you want?'

Without waiting for an invitation, Aleena climbs the ramp and directs the villager to place the tray onto a cargo crate just inside the ship. She smiles at the man. 'Thank you. Go and join the others.'

He glances at Gryffin before he nods at Aleena and disappears along the track back to the village. Aleena points to the crates against the far wall. 'Would you kindly pull over two more crates?'

'What?'

'Crates. Unless you would prefer to sit on the floor.'

He does as he's told and sits down opposite her. 'What do you want?'

She pulls the cloth off the tray to reveal more food than he's seen in months. 'Since you were keen to remain on the ship, I thought I would bring some of the food to you.'

'I don't want anything.'

She shrugs as she picks up a chunk of bread and pops it in her mouth. After chewing for a moment she swallows and smiles. 'My famous cheese bread. You really should try some.'

'I don't want anything,' he repeats.

'My deal with you was to supply each of the Nomad

on this ship with food. You are one of those Nomad. Eat.'

Gryffin eyes the food suspiciously.

'I just ate some bread. Try that if you do not trust the rest.'

Gryffin reaches out and takes a piece of the offered bread. She's right. It's pretty damn good.

'Before I forget.' She removes his necklace from around her neck and places it on the crate in front of him. 'I must return this to you.'

He fastens it in place, strangely comforted by the feel of it around his neck again. The platinum griffin is more than just his namesake. It's the only link to his life before the Scientist took him. He vaguely remembers the dark-haired woman who gave it to him, but he doesn't have a clue who she is or why she gave it to him.

'How is your wound? And before you respond, I would like an answer other than 'fine."

He stops chewing and looks across at her. 'You're not afraid of me.'

She takes a drink from her glass before responding. 'Is that a question or a statement?'

'Both.'

'I have a healthy respect for the fact you could kill me whenever you feel the urge.'

'I'm not going to kill you.'

'It will take a little more than a worded confirmation to believe you. Your actions throughout our... partnership will say more to me. But to answer your question, no. I do not fear you as such. Are you disappointed by that?'

Gryffin picks up another piece of bread as he looks towards the village. He's not used to being spoken to like this. Giving and receiving orders is as far as conversation goes for him. Having a chat over dinner is something he's only done with Rayde, and that was usually a one-sided thing.

'I have the distinct impression you are not fond of answering questions, Captain. If we are to work together, it would be helpful to get to know each other a little better.'

'Why?'

She laughs at his question. 'Oh my. It appears I have my work cut out for me. Knowing each other better will help us work better together. You know each of your crew.' She pauses at the look of confusion on his face. 'Or perhaps not. Very well, would you care to share your name with me yet? I would prefer that to calling you 'captain' all the time.' He raises an eyebrow and she sighs loudly. 'Have you been told you are an infuriating man, Captain?'

The silence continues for a few minutes as they eat. He's grateful she's not pushing for conversation. This entire situation is so alien to him. 'I've got some tools and scrap metal crated up for you. I'll get it brought to the town centre before we leave tomorrow.'

'Thank you. I trust the food I had delivered will be sufficient?'

Gryffin nods. Having fresh fruit, vegetables and

bread in their store is a rarity. It'll make a nice change from ration bars and whatever the food dispensers on *Ares* can produce. He gestures to a large rectangular box at the far side of the bay. 'That's a transmitter. We'll leave it here after we go. It'll transmit a Nomad signal. Anyone comes near the planet and they'll pick it up. Should encourage them to keep away.'

'I appreciate that. How can I contact you if there are any problems?'

He gets up and takes the unit from the top of the box. He places it on the crate in front of her. 'You need anything you can contact *Ares* on that. The power supply will last for a few months. Same with the transmitter. We'll be back to recharge them before they run out.'

Aleena examines the unit and laughs.

'What?'

'If someone had told me a few days ago I would be having dinner with a Nomad who came to raid the colony, then saved it, I would most likely have laughed at them. How did we come from there to here? It is quite an achievement.'

'Making the best of a bad situation.'

'Indeed. I believe we can make this a beneficial partnership - for the Ultarans and the Nomad.'

'I'm taking a risk doing this. It better be beneficial. My crew will have my head otherwise.'

Alena looks at him strangely. 'I will have to make sure that does not happen. I have contacted quite a few of the neighbouring colonies. If this agreement works out, there are more who would be interested in a similar deal - with the Nomad acting as intermediaries. There could also be other colonies willing to pay for protection. This agreement with Ultar could very well be the first of many.'

'See how it goes with us first.'

'Agreed.' Aleena holds up her glass. 'Shall we toast to it?'

Gryffin stares at his glass for a minute before he finally picks it up and taps it against hers. 'To the future, Captain.'

Gryffin doesn't reply. He's got to convince Rayde before he can even consider the future of this agreement. If given a choice, he'd have a rerun with the Slavers instead of that conversation.

16

'How did the raid go on Ultar?'

Gryffin doesn't want to have this discussion with Rayde yet, but he has little choice. 'I made a deal with the leader. In return for-'

'I know what you damn well agreed to. I read your report and I have to admit, I'm more than a little confused. You do realise Nomad don't deal?'

'The deal made sense.'

Rayde gets up and paces the room as he laughs to himself. 'Made sense. Well, that's that then. Nothing else to discuss.'

'We can make some credits this way. Maybe get

enough to fix the ships.'

'And while we're at it how about we get a nice little house on Ultar and raise pigs. I mean, are you out of your damn mind, son? This is a terrible idea. You should have just killed her and left it at that.'

'There was no need to kill her.'

Rayde pulls out his knife, a large blade with an ornate handle that he took from his first kill. He twirls it in his hand and Gryffin's stomach lurches. He knows what's coming next.

'You didn't use the implant, did you.' The statement doesn't need to be answered so Gryffin keeps quiet. 'I have to admit I'm a little disappointed. Perhaps if you had, you wouldn't have made this disastrous mistake. I thought you agreed with me?'

'I do, sir.'

'Then why do you still argue with me? I have given you *Ares* because I thought you were the right Nomad for the role. Did I make a mistake?'

'No. I didn't need the implant.'

'Perhaps, but if you did use it, we would not be having this discussion.' He stops pacing and Gryffin takes a step back. 'Have you been using it regularly?'

Gryffin's initial reaction is to lie, but it would just make things worse. 'Only if I really need to.'

'Sounds like we have different views on when you need to use it. How many times do I have to say this to you before it gets through that skull of yours? It's a part of you - a fucking big one. Ignoring it won't do you any favours.'

'I don't want anything to do with it.' Gryffin grimaces as the words spill out before he can stop them.

'What makes you think you have a choice!' Rayde pauses and runs his hand through his hair as he blows out a long breath. 'Why are you so insistent on denying what you are? You are a cyborg. Pretending to be something else is a waste of time and a waste of an opportunity. We have a chance to make the Nomad a formidable group. With a virtually unstoppable captain at the helm of our main ship, no one would dare defy us.' Rayde places a hand on Gryffin's shoulder. 'C'mon, son. Work with me. You owe me that much at least. Stop holding back.'

Gryffin nods slowly as he tries to ignore the sinking feeling in his stomach. 'Yes, sir.' He closes his eyes and tries to get the implant to change his eyes, but nothing happens. He knows a part of the problem is with him. He hates when it has control of him. Now he has partial hold of the reins, he's not eager to let go again.

'Anything?' Rayde asks. Gryffin shakes his head and braces for what he knows is coming. Rayde pushes the handle of his blade against the bandage on Gryffin's stomach. 'Let it out, son.'

Not getting the desired effect, Rayde pushes harder and Gryffin grunts as the stitches rupture. He feels the implant coming to the forefront, then remembers what he did on Ultar - focusing on the pain to stop the implant. He ignores the taunts of encouragement from Rayde and directs all his attention on the wound. The deep throb of the newly opened injury is intense as Rayde pushes against it. Gryffin smiles to himself as he feels his grip on the implant increase. A few deep breaths later, he opens his eyes to face a very confused Rayde.

'What the fuck did you just do?'

17

Rayde glares at Gryffin as he wipes the blood from the handle of his knife. 'I think you owe me an explanation, son.'

'I learnt to control it.'

Rayde scrutinises him in silence for a minute. 'You learnt to control it? I thought you could already control it. I thought that's what all our training was for.'

'If I can stop it from taking over even a few times, that's good, right?'

'Is it?'

'I don't want my crew thinking I could lose control

and kill one of them. I need to be able to hold it back... well, some of the time.'

Rayde studies him as he polishes his blade. 'Is that right. Forgive me but I'm not seeing how that'll benefit the Nomad as a whole. You need to be doing the exact opposite. Best you stop this foolishness and get back to some serious, useful training.'

Gryffin doesn't respond. The last thing he wants to do is let go of whatever small grasp on the implant he's managed to get. Rayde puts the knife down and crosses his arms over his chest. 'So, I'm guessing this fucking ridiculous trade deal came after your newly learnt control. That explains a lot. I just have one question. What gives you the lofty impression you know how to do things better than those before you? I've been a Nomad my whole life - I know the way things should be done. It's been that way for years.'

'She asked me to work with them. She wants protection.'

'Give me a fucking break. You should be attacking them!' He sits back in his chair and sighs. 'Have you heard yourself?' He taps the side of his head. 'There must be something lose up there if you're taking *Ares* in this direction.'

'They're going to pay us. We need the credits.'

Rayde slams his fist against the arm of the chair. 'Not at the risk of Nomad lives! Raid the colonies and take the credits, dammit!'

'That's a bigger risk than trading.'

Rayde rubs his forehead and curses under his

breath. 'I want my medic, Klay, to give you a thorough examination. There's obviously something wrong.'

'No.' He can't remember ever saying that to Rayde before.

Rayde freezes and slowly lifts his head. 'What was that, boy?'

'I'm not malfunctioning. I don't need to be checked. The deal with Ultar stands.'

Rayde smiles, but it's far from cheery. 'Is that so?'

'You put me in charge of *Ares*. This is the way we're doing things.'

Rayde nods once and gets to his feet, the blade in his hand again. 'I'm thinking I may have made a mistake. You're clearly not ready for the responsibility of command. I'll take back *Ares* – just until you're checked out to make sure something hasn't come loose in that head of yours. Now you can either walk to *Kratos* or I can drag you there myself.'

'I'm not going anywhere.'

Rayde attacks before Gryffin can convince himself to react. The first punch is hard and knocks him to one knee. Gryffin's one of the best fighters on board, but this is Rayde. This is the man who saved him from hell. There's no way he can fight back.

'You were weak when I found you. I thought I'd made you strong, made you a fighter. Yet here you are making friends with the locals. Look at you now! You're still cowering in a corner.'

Gryffin tries to shield his face from the blows but they keep coming, hard and fast. After a few minutes,

Rayde stops, gasping for breath. Gryffin slumps back against the wall and wipes the blood from of his eye.

Rayde leans against the desk and cleans his hands on his trousers. He glares down at him, still trying to get his breathing under control. The silence stretches on until Rayde points a thick finger at him. 'You fucked up, Gryffin. This isn't what I had planned for that pathetic boy I found.'

As he watches the older man sharpen the blade on the buckle of his belt, something changes inside him. Rayde's right. He's not that little boy anymore. Thanks to Rayde, he's strong, fit, and more than capable of standing up for himself. How can he expect his crew to have any respect for him if he can't fight for himself?

Rayde pauses as Gryffin pushes to his feet. He lets the implant in his head have a little freedom, turning his eyes purple. Even though the feeling turns his stomach, he needs it if he's going to get through this without being cut open again.

'Care to tell me what you're doing?' Rayde asks.

'Get off my ship.'

Rayde laughs harshly. 'Now I know there's something wrong in your head. You're forgetting your place, son.'

'No, you are. I'm the captain of *Ares* now - not you. You want to take her from me, you're going to have to do it by force. Not sure how that'll work out for you.'

'I'm the High Commander. You answer to me.'

'For now.' The words pop out before Gryffin knows what he's saying. Is he seriously going to unseat

Rayde? The position of High Commander was something he never considered for himself - until that moment.

'You'd take my fucking role from me?' he scoffs.

'That's what you want, right? You want an heir, someone to take over after you.'

'My way! Not like this. Not with trading. Not by destroying everything the Nomad are.'

Gryffin shrugs. '*Ares* is trading. My decision - not yours. If you don't like it I'll pull the ship out of the group, set up on my own.'

Rayde's eyes open wide and he takes a step back like he's been struck. His fist tightens around the blade as he glares at Gryffin with contempt. Gryffin braces himself for the impact, sure the blade will be heading his way. 'After everything-'

'Yes. I'll always owe you for saving me, but I'm done being a punching bag. You need to back off. Let me run my ship my way.'

Rayde is quiet for a long time. Gryffin holds his stance, leaving the implant in control so he doesn't give Rayde any reason to doubt him. Rayde finally sheaths his blade and clasps his hands in front of him. 'I thought we had an understanding, but I guess I've only got myself to blame. Like you so clearly put it; you're only doing what I taught you to do - being strong and unwavering in your actions. I suppose I should be proud...'

He shrugs, leaving the sentence unfinished. Gryffin knows he's just changed their relationship forever but it's too late to back down now. If he's to have any chance of surviving as Captain he needs to act like one. 'Now, you can either walk to *Kratos* or I can drag you there myself.'

Rayde smile is cold as Gryffin repeats his own words back to him. As soon as the door closes behind Rayde, Gryffin drops into the chair and stares at the far wall. What the hell has he just done?

18

'Bloody hell, sir! What happened to you?'

Sayber follows Gryffin into his small bathroom and leans against the door frame. Gryffin picks up the blood-soaked cloth and goes back to cleaning his face. 'Disagreement with Rayde.'

'And he did that to you? Remind me not to disagree with him. Explains why he left in a bit of a hurry.' Sayber's eyes wander down Gryffin's back, locking on the various scars left by Rayde over the years. 'You going to tell me why he beat you to a pulp?'

'What do you want, Sayber?' He's not going to get into the fight with Rayde. The whole messed up situation is something he'd prefer to keep to himself.

'Well, after the High Commander left in a whirlwind of hostility, I thought I'd check if you plan to ditch the trades or keep them going?'

Gryffin winces as he presses a little too hard on a cut over his eye. 'Rayde wants us to stop.'

'Yeah, I kinda got that from all the blood. What about you?'

Gryffin drops the cloth into the sink and rests his hands on the cool surface. He's decided to continue with the trades, but as soon as he gives the order, there's no going back. He'll be working against the man who rescued him, who gave him a life. It would be the biggest knife in the back he could give Rayde. It would also disrespect him to continue the way they've been going for years. Rayde trained him hard to never back down. Consider your options and stick with the plan of attack. That's exactly what he's doing.

'We're trading.'

'Understood, sir.'

'You think the crew will have a problem?'

'Does it matter?'

'Of course it damn well matters.'

'It's going to be mixed, but that's a guess. We've been doing things like this since the Nomad was formed. Of course there'll be a few who will be seriously pissed off with any change. They accepted you as Captain though. That's got to give you some confidence.'

'That was with Rayde's backing. We do this, we're

alone.'

'Nomad don't fly in a group. We're always alone. The only way you'll be able to convince the doubters is by not getting us killed in the next few weeks and bringing in some credits.'

'Is that all? '

'Never said it would be an easy task, sir.'

'We within range of Ultar yet?'

'In about an hour.'

'Let me know when I can talk to Aleena. Might be time to pull in a few favours. See if anyone else wants to deal. Get more credits coming in.'

Sayber nods and leaves Gryffin to clean up the rest of Rayde's work from his body. He meets his reflection in the mirror and curses when purple eyes look back at him. He splashes cold water on his face, trying to snap himself out of the cycle. This is the last time Rayde will do this to him. It's the last time Rayde will use pain to bring the implant out. His eyes obey, dark blue winning the fight for dominance. Gryffin smiles. A new direction for the Nomad and new direction for him. All he has to do is prove to Rayde that he hasn't screwed up the Nomad for good.

ARES

An hour later, Gryffin sits down at his desk and grimaces at his reflection in the blank screen. He pulls some hair forward, covering the cut over his eye. Nothing he can do to hide the bruising on his face.

Aleena appears on the screen, and her smile fades when she notices the bruises. 'Whatever happened to you?'

'Training drone kicked my ass.'

'Perhaps we should hire one of these drones to protect us instead.' She smiles, but he's not in the mood to play along.

'What you said - about other colonies and trading. That still stand?'

'Of course. Would you like me to give you details of the leaders I've been speaking to?'

'Don't want to give my contact codes to half the Sector. I'd prefer to go through you for now. You good with that?'

She nods. 'If you are sure you trust me with passing on your terms.'

'I distrust you less than most people I deal with.'

Aleena stares at him before she shakes her head. 'You have a way with compliments, Captain. How many do you wish me to contact?'

'How many you got?'

'Three ready to trade. Another four perhaps who will need a little more proof you and your men can keep to your side of the agreement.'

Better numbers than he thought. If he can sign on the three colonies now, they'll be in a sound position. 'Start with the ones ready to go. Once the others see I won't bleed them dry, they might follow.'

'Beautiful imagery, Captain. Leave it with me. I will contact them later today.'

Gryffin glances at his comms unit. 'Hang on, Aleena. What is it, Sayber?'

'Need you on the command deck.'

'On my way.' He cuts the connection and addresses Aleena again. 'I'm under pressure to prove the trades work. If this backfires I won't have a choice but to go back to the old ways. Understood?'

'I understand perfectly.'

'Let me know how you get on.' He cuts the connection and uses the desk to push himself to his feet. He takes a deep breath and smiles to himself as his ribs protest. Rayde did a real number on him, but it won't be happening again. He'll gladly take the bruises now if it means he has gained a little control – not just of the implant, but of his life. That's worth a little pain.

∞

Sayber stares at the door to Gryffin's office, but the damn thing is still closed. What the hell is taking him so long? Eventually, the captain emerges, one hand pressed to his side as he slowly crosses the deck. 'What's the problem?'

'The station at Milara One is under attack. Sounds like Rogues.'

Gryffin checks the viewscreen and frowns at Sayber. 'What?'

'Milara One is under attack. Will I alter our course? We could be there in an hour max.'

'Why the hell would we alter course? We're not getting involved.'

'But, sir. We've traded with the station in the past. We have allies there.'

Gryffin sucks in a breath as he lowers into his command chair and rubs his bruised jaw. 'We've traded there twice. They're not allies. You called me out for this?'

'Sir, the station is-'

'The station is nothing to us. The last time we were there a local gang attacked us. It's a dump filled with the dregs of the Sector.' Sayber curses and Gryffin glares at him 'What the hell is your problem, Commander?'

'Like I said, we have allies there. I strongly recommend we go and lend a hand. This is a big mistake, sir.'

'Let me make this clear, Commander. I'm not putting the ship and crew in danger to save the necks of some petty thieves and Slavers.'

'I have allies there. I'm asking you to please change course.'

'And I'm saying no. The station is under attack now. In the hour it takes to get there the damage will be done.'

'So that's it? We just ignore them? What if it was *Ares* under attack. You'd want someone to hear you and help. We need to go!'

Gryffin's eye changes colour which is usually enough for Sayber to take a step back, but not this time. This time he's not backing down. This time it's personal.

'Permission to take a transport.'

'Denied.'

'But-'

'Take five, Commander.'

'Sir-'

'You get the hell off my command deck or I'll remove you myself and it'll be a one-way trip. Understood?'

Sayber's jaw clenches as he fights to control his tongue. Arguing will force Gryffin to act and he knows damn well he won't come out of that in one piece. With the eyes of the crew burning into him, he nods briskly and turns away from Gryffin before he signs his death sentence.

Once he's alone in his quarters, he beats the wall with his fists and screams until his throat is raw. Never in his life has he felt so helpless, so powerless to do a damn thing for someone he cares about.

Like Gryffin said, they had only traded with the station twice, but he had been with Hetta both times. Their relationship was very new and it was far too early to say if it would have had a future. Now he'd never know. It doesn't matter that Gryffin's right. By the time they reach the station, the damage would be done. But not doing anything at all is more than he can bear.

She could be hurt, hoping he'd come to help them. Instead, he was forced to do fuck all. He respected Gryffin as a captain, but never fully trusted him. How could he? How could anyone when no one knew exactly what he was or what he was designed to do. Too much was unknown and that could only spell trouble. Nothing he could do about it. Just like there's nothing he can do to save Hetta. Nothing except keep his fingers crossed and hope for the best.

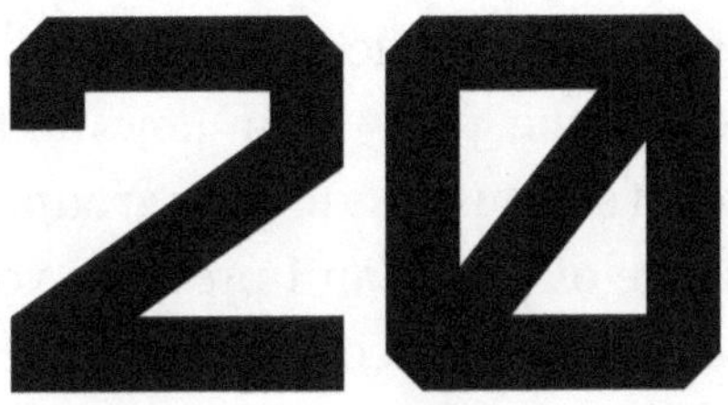

ULTAR

Aleena smiles as the Nomad battleship lands in the meadow beside the lake. The rear ramp lowers and her smile widens as Gryffin walks down and approaches her. Since their last visit, the Nomad have acquired new uniforms. Instead of the threadbare mismatched outfits they wore when they landed to raid, Gryffin and his team are all wearing black. Leather trousers, high boots, and leather jackets are matched with heavy holsters strapped to their waists and legs holding quite an arsenal.

He stops beside her and gestures behind him. 'Got the supplies you wanted.'

'Welcome back, Captain. How are you?'

He frowns, ignores her question and signals to his men. 'Bring the delivery to the town hall.'

Aleena shakes her head. 'I asked, how are you?'

'Fine.' Aleena laughs and he frowns at her. 'What the hell is so funny?'

'Not funny, just predictable, Captain. I must say, you look quite the part. Your new uniforms add a certain level of seriousness to your group. Not that you need any more of that. Can I presume you have been to the colony I suggested? I would recognise their craftsmanship anywhere.'

'Uniforms were payment for trading.'

'I see. How many colonies do you deal with now?'

'More than we did.'

She sighs and turns away. 'Would you care to walk with me?'

'Where?'

'To the tunnels. We have recently uncovered an entrance just outside the village. It has revealed something I would value your opinion on.' He nods and walks beside her in silence to the village. She attempts small talk but apart from a few nods or grunts, he manages to keep the conversation one-sided.

Aleena had been keeping close contact with all the colony leaders she had signed up with the Nomad. A few had taken a little persuasion to willingly allow a Nomad vessel on their world, but the captain and his men had proved themselves. Within a few weeks of the third deal being agreed, a Slaver ship had ignored the beacon and landed on one of the worlds. Thankfully, *Ares* had been in the area and shown them, in no uncertain terms, how much of a mistake that was.

The actions of Gryffin and his crew had sealed the deal with the remaining doubters. It was better to be aligned with a group like the Nomad than face Slavers and other unscrupulous groups with no protection.

She looks across at him and smiles. 'I heard you and your men have been busy. Were any of you injured when you fought the Slaver ship?'

He shakes his head. 'Didn't take a lot of persuasion to get them to back off. The few we left alive will have gone back to the others and told them what happened. Should persuade any other ships to watch out for the Nomad beacons orbiting colonies.'

'I have been approached by two more colonies who wish to speak to you.'

'Fine. Send the details through and I'll have a look.' He looks down at her when she laughs. 'What?'

'When I broached the subject of trading with you I never expected it would grow as it has.'

'I didn't either.'

'So I presume you have proved to your superior and the others in the group that this was a good idea.'

He takes a deep breath and rubs the side of the metal around his eye. After many conversations with the captain, she knows that is something he does when he is deciding what to say. Perhaps the deals had not been so readily accepted by whoever he reports to.

'Yeah. No complaints.'

Aleena nods but knows without a doubt he is keeping something from her.

∞

Gryffin looks around the vast cavern and can't help but be impressed. The man-made cave extends deep underground and would easily fit *Ares* along with quite a few transports. Three rusted tracks lead from deep collection pits at the base of the lift and snake away into the darkness of the adjoining tunnels. At the end of each track sits a heavy, steel, cage-like lift. Each one has seen better days, the tattered rope connecting them to the upper shaft rotted away with time. Dozens of wooden crates line the far wall. Most have burst, spilling their contents on the floor. 'Are there more tunnels?'

'We believe they extend much further but have yet to explore beyond a few miles. Much of the records were destroyed when the town hall flooded during a rainstorm a few years ago. From what I remember from my grandfather, the mines were truly vast.'

Gryffin picks up a piece of the black rock. The fine dust coats his glove. 'What is it?'

'A natural fuel source. The mines were closed when my grandfather was a child. The supply had been exhausted. In the space of a few weeks, the locals were out of work, had no income and no future. A few Ultarans had moved to farming when they became too frail to work down here. The practice spread and we grew into what we are today.'

'There another way in?'

She nods and walks over to the wall behind the crates. Aleena pulls a plank of wood from the wall to expose yet more wood behind it. 'There are two doors behind this. They open into the woods. The track has been taken back by the forest, but it would not take much to uncover it. Why do you ask?'

'I don't want the rest of my crew to know about this place.'

'Why ever not?'

'How many of your people know?'

She shrugs. 'A few dozen Ultarans, but I fail to see what the issue is.'

'Something like this could be invaluable.'

'For what?'

The room suddenly tilts and Gryffin reaches out a hand to steady himself, regaining his footing before he lands on the ground. His vision swims and throws the room on its side again.

Aleena hurries over to him. 'Captain?'

He wants to reply with his usual *I'm fine* but he's far from it. The control implant has had enough of him silencing it and is forcing its way out. In a desperate attempt to keep it at bay, Gryffin slams his arm against the rock wall. The pain registers, but it's not enough. The control implant is coming out and there's fuck all he can do about it.

He doubles over as the invisible red hot spike works

its way through his chest implant, stealing the air from his lungs before it moves up to his head to settle behind his eyes in a sickening, vice-like grip of pressure.

Aleena touches his shoulder and speaks to him but he barely hears what she's saying. He hasn't had an attack like this for months. What the hell was he thinking coming down here alone? He looks around the cavern, desperate to find something to hold him while the implant has him. The lifts are his best bet. 'The implant in my head is going to take over. You need to lock me in there.'

She glances over at the lift cages then back at him. 'I do not understand? Take over what?'

'Just lock me in there! I'm going to be a big fucking problem if you don't.'

Whether it's his statement or the look in his eyes that convinces her, Aleena hurries over to the nearest cage and pulls at the door. After a few attempts, the rusted hinges scream into submission as she yanks it open. Gryffin stumbles in as the pain reaches a nearly unbearable level. He falls to the ground, clutching his head to stop it from splitting open. 'Chain my wrists.'

She drags an old pile of chains over to the cage along with a wooden box of padlocks. As she untangles the chains, Gryffin takes his guns and knife from his belt and places them on the ground outside the bars. Aleena hands Gryffin two lengths of chain which he wraps around his wrists as the other ends are secured to the bars of the makeshift cell. Gryffin clicks the locks in place. 'Chain the gate closed.'

He screams as invisible hands grip the top of his skull, squeezing and twisting it until he's convinced it's going to pop off. He glances up at the gates and is relieved to see Aleena twisting a thick chain in place. She secures it with a heavily rusty padlock, clicking it closed before stepping away again.

'I will lock the doors to the cavern then notify your people.

'No! Don't. Damn it, don't tell my crew. Please.'

Aleena stares at him for a few seconds then nods. 'Very well.' She hurries out of the cavern and returns a few moments later. 'I have sealed the doors and told my people we are in a meeting and must not be disturbed. What can I do to help, Captain?'

'Get the hell of here,' he replies through clenched teeth.

'I am not leaving you alone.'

'There's nothing you can do. Get away from the cage and leave me alone. Now!' He doesn't know if she does as he demands or not. He couldn't really care less. The control implant has him and it wants out of the cage.

21

Aleena wraps her arms around herself as she stares at the unconscious Nomad leader. The captain had shouted, screamed, and fought to get out of his bonds for close to an hour and Aleena had remained motionless at the far side of the cavern unable to do anything to help. So far none of the Nomad had come looking for him. They were still busy with the supplies and had not needed to disturb him.

The tears had stopped running down Aleena's face after the first thirty minutes. She may not comprehend what is happening to the Nomad leader but she recognises the pain in his face. While most of the shouts and protests had been born from uncontrollable rage, some came from pain. When not pulling at the chains securing him, he would clutch his head and release a roar of pain which Aleena has never heard before nor wants to hear again.

How can she have a normal conversation with him one moment then have to lock him in a cage the next? What could possibly be in his head to cause such an extreme reaction? For the first time since she met him, a disturbing thought settles and refuses to leave. She had assumed he had requested the modifications be done to him. What if that were not the case? Perhaps they had been fitted to him without his consent. The thought alone sends an icy chill up her spine. She would prefer to believe anything but that.

She breathes a sigh of relief as he opens his eyes, winces, then closes them again.

'Captain?'

He groans and peers across at her through half-closed eyes. The heavy chains drag along the ground as he pushes himself on to his back. He lies on the dusty floor, breathing heavily. 'The... crew?'

She gets to her feet and slowly approaches the cage. 'Still busy unloading the supplies. No one is aware of what happened. I am including myself in that statement of course.'

He rolls away from her and retches in the corner before crashing down on to his back again. 'Sorry.'

Aleena smiles and shakes her head. 'No need for apologies. Is there anything I can get you?'

He lifts his wrist off the ground and rattles the chain. 'The key?' Aleena pauses and he rolls on his side to face her. He closes his eyes and his brow furrows briefly. 'It's finished. I'm not a threat anymore.'

'You are always a threat, Captain. That is why you are protecting us. What exactly is finished? I have watched you for the last hour and I am at a loss for words. I would like an explanation.'

She crouches down in front of the cage and waits for a response. When he opens his eyes he seems to have trouble focusing. 'My eyesight is going.'

'I do not understand?'

He looks towards her but not at her. 'The implant... it knocks my eyes off for thirty minutes to an hour. I'll be blind until the... until it all comes back again.'

'Very well. I will unlock you and we can go back to my house. You can rest until your eyesight returns, perhaps get cleaned up and we can talk. It will give you time to get yourself together before you return to your ship.'

Fully expecting a firm refusal, Aleena is pleasantly surprised when he nods and holds his wrist up again. 'Key.'

In response, she lifts a small metal box from the floor. He stares blankly ahead of him, unable to see so she rattles the box containing dozens of similarly sized keys. 'This may take some time, Captain.'

22

Aleena places more wood on the fire and settles into her favourite chair by the window as she stares into her tea. The captain had called *Ares* and told his crew he would be another hour or so. He was mid negotiations about more trade deals and needed time to finish things. Aleena does not know how he managed to put enough strength in his voice to fool his crew. Whatever had happened in the tunnels had taken its toll on him.

After spending quite some time trying each key in the numerous locks securing him, they had finally released him and dragged him to the waiting cart.

Adamant that his crew did not see him, Gryffin had remained under a cover in the back while she guided the horse drawn cart back to her house. The journey had not been more than ten minutes, but the captain had struggled to remain conscious. His eyesight had completely gone or 'shut down' as he put it, by the time they reached the house. With the last of his strength dwindling, he crawled up the stairs and stumbled into the spare bedroom.

She helped him on the small bed and left him alone while she fetched some water. When she returned a short while later, she found him asleep. His large body seemed to dwarf the bed, his dark clothes and weapon holsters a stark contrast to the floral patchwork quilt under him.

With nothing else to do, she busied herself preparing some fish stew. She would rather keep busy than let her mind wander to the unsettling questions she has about the Nomad captain.

She has just put the stew in the cooker when she hears water running in the upstairs shower. Shortly afterwards heavy, if not slightly unsteady footsteps move down the stairs. He slowly makes his way over to the chair opposite hers and collapses into it. He rests his head against the back and closes his eyes.

Without the layer of dirt on his face, his skin is pale and an unhealthy shade of grey. Red, raw lesions surround his wrist and there's a cut on his forehead from where he banged it against the bars of the makeshift cage. Without saying anything, Aleena takes the medical kit from beside her chair and kneels in front of him. 'May I clean your wounds?'

He lifts his head and looks from her to his wrist then back again. She holds his gaze, determined not to back down. After a long wait, he finally answers. 'I don't like people touching me.'

'Why not?'

'I just don't.'

'Very well. I will just use a swab, Captain.' Careful to keep her hand away from his flesh, she gently dabs at the wound, cleaning it as best she can. 'Captain, I would like to know exactly what that was back there.'

He looks at the fire and brushes the wet hair from his face. The awkward silence stretches on so long she is sure he is never going to respond to her question. She puts the used swab in the bowl and reaches for a bandage. He sits forward and, with some difficulty, pulls his t-shirt off.

Aleena slumps back on her haunches and stares at the intricate path of metal attached to his toned chest. The large W shaped piece stretches from under each armpit, below the waistband of his trousers and up the centre of his chest. Technology and Aleena are not the best of friends but she can make out connectors of sorts scattered along the length of the piece. Upon closer inspection, she realises the metalwork is embedded in his skin, not attached to the surface.

Aleena meets his eyes then moves her attention to the other metalwork around his eye. More scars spread out from the smooth metal leaving the skin rough and uneven. A series of screws are visible around the edge of the metal, presumably to attach the implant to his flesh... or bone. The thought turns her stomach. She looks down at his metal arm and sees similar scaring where the appendage meets with his skin. Whatever happened to him, it was not a kind or gentle procedure. The realisation hits her, momentarily throwing her off balance. 'You did not get these modifications by choice.'

He slumps back in the chair and focuses on the fire again. 'My parents sold me to a scientist when I was a kid. He used me as his test subject in his cyborg project. I was there for years before the Nomad found me and let me join *Ares*. There's something in my head. Some sort of implant or program. The Nomad still don't fully know what it does or what it's meant to do. All I know is I'm always fighting to keep it under control.'

His words hit Aleena like a blow to the chest. She swallows to moisten her throat but it does little good. 'That is what you meant when we were in the lake. You said you were trying not to kill me.'

He nods. 'I have control of it most of the time, but now and again, it retaliates and takes over. I get a few minutes warning when that's going to happen. There's a cell on *Ares* for when I'm a threat. First time it's happened off the ship.'

Aleena cannot imagine what it must be like for him to live with a cell at the ready in case he needs to be contained. With no words suitable to fill the silence, she watches him as he stares into the fire. It may be due to the fact he is tired, but she can see true emotion on his face for the first time since she met him. If it were any other party opposite her she would have wrapped her arms around them and held them close. Not a course of action the Nomad captain would appreciate or accept - of that she has no doubt. Instead, she reaches out to the small table beside her chair and gathers the tools. 'May I see your injured wrist?'

He frowns and pulls his attention away from the fire. 'What?'

'I need to measure it.' She holds up the strip of leather in her hand. 'I would imagine your crew would have a few questions if they see a bandage. This will cover the wound.'

He glances down at his wrist then back at Aleena before he leans forward and slowly offers her his arm. She wraps the leather strap gently around his wrist, marks where the edges meet then gets to work cutting it to size and fixing rivets to the leather as fasteners. When finished, she wraps it around his wrist again and secures the thick band over the bandaged wound. She examines her work, pleased that the leather completely covers any sign of a wound. 'That should do the job nicely. Does it feel comfortable?'

'It's good. I should get back to *Ares*.' He pushes to his feet but grabs on to the back of the chair as his balance waivers.

'Please stay, Captain. You need to rest before you go

back.'

'I don't need to rest. They'll come looking for me soon.'

'Do the Nomad hurt you?'

He freezes and frowns at her. 'What the hell do you mean by that?'

She tucks her arms around herself, unable to rid her body of the chills that have settled since he began talking. 'You have quite a few serious scars on your chest and arms.'

'They saved my life.'

'That does not answer my question.'

He steps closer to her, standing well over two heads taller than her as he stares down at her. 'We're trade partners - not friends. I only told you about my implants because of what happened today. Don't make me regret that decision.'

His threat would have been far more effective if his legs had continued to support his weight. Instead, the captain falls against the wall and slowly slides to the ground as his skin tone turns a sickly shade of green. Aleena rushes into the kitchen, fetches the bucket by the door and places it in front of him just in time. He curses and rubs a trembling hand over his face as he fights to get control of his body. Aleena leaves him to deal with his sickness in private, busing herself in the kitchen until he appears at the doorway. She hands him a glass of water which he accepts with a weak smile. 'How do you feel?'

'It takes a few hours to get over it.'

She squeezes his arm then drops her hand when he recoils and backs away from her. 'I was going to offer you some fish stew but I do not think that would be a good idea.' He shakes his head and reaches for his shirt. 'Captain, I appreciate you telling me. I assure you it will go no further and I will not press you for more information on the matter. However, I want you to know that you can talk to me if you need to.'

He tilts his head to the side as he frowns at her. 'I should go.'

Aleena decides it would be prudent to change the subject as she follows him back to the main reception room. 'Why not tell them about the tunnels?'

'Having tunnels like that under the colony is invaluable. I need you to explore them with a few trustworthy people. Map everything. Check your archives and collect all data about the tunnels. Keep it hidden. The fewer people who know about them the better.'

'Of course. I will begin the process in the morning.' She walks him to the door. The night has drawn in, bringing with it heavy rain that collects in puddles on her gravel pathway. He slips his jacket on as he steps under the porch. 'Are you forgetting something?' She points to his guns and knife on the table by the door. 'I would prefer you take these with you.'

He frowns at the weapons. 'That would have been hard to explain.'

'Indeed.'

Gryffin slides them into their holsters, leaning

down to adjust the weapon on his leg. Before she can stop herself, she kisses him on the cheek. Gryffin straightens and frowns at her. 'What the hell was that for?'

'Friendship, Captain.'

He looks out into the rain briefly before he turns back to her. 'Gryffin.'

'Excuse me?'

'My name is Gryffin,' he says as he disappears into the night.

PART 2

1 YEAR LATER

GRYFFIN – 30 YEARS OLD
BRAY – 25 YEARS OLD

23

Gryffin closes the comms with Rayde and rubs his forehead. Since their disagreement last year on the trade deals, their relationship had been tense. The group is doing a hell of a lot better from the trades and for the first time in as long as he can remember, the ship and crew looks healthy and are in one piece. Still wasn't good enough for Rayde though. He's hoping time will help put things right between them but until then he'll have to deal with the cold front.

He had planned on meeting with another Nomad ship a few days travel from their location but changed his mind. They've been on the move non-stop for weeks. He's worn out and his men need a break from the ship. Maybe a few days on Ultar will recharge everyone.

He opens his mouth to give the order to change coordinates when Sayber storms up the stairs and stops in front of him. He points his gun at Gryffin and fires. It takes Gryffin longer than it should to react but his body kicks into gear, moving him to the side. Instead of hitting his ocular implant, the round embeds itself the back of his command chair.

'Lock down the command deck!' he roars as he pulls his gun out.

The doors to the deck slide shut to seal them inside. Alarms scream to life as the ship runs through emergency lockdown procedures. Gryffin watches in horror as three Nomad with Sayber fire on other crew, trying to clear any resistance. Gryffin grabs the nearest man to him and pulls him to the ground before he's taken down.

For the next minute, Gryffin and his Nomad exchange fire with Sayber and his Nomad. Stray rounds puncture systems, sending sparks and smoke spewing into the room. More alarms join with the main emergency alarm adding their screech to the smoke and chaos.

'Sayber! What the fuck are you doing?'

'Think that would be clear. I'm taking *Ares*. Drop your weapons and come out. I don't want any more Nomad dying because of this.'

Gryffin curses as he reloads his gun. He looks down

at the Nomad lying at his feet. It's too late for promises like that. 'You turned the crew?'

'Just enough. Surrender, Gryffin. It's the only way to save the rest.' Sayber's rambling is cut off as a support holding a roof panel in place creaks and gives way, dropping a heavy sheet of metal to the floor.

'Fucker is messing up my ship,' Gryffin mutters to himself as he aims and takes down another of Sayber's men.

'Gryffin! Only one of us is getting off the deck. My men are outside waiting to come in. Why don't you make this easy and go down without a fight? For once do the right thing.'

Sayber's last man drops as Gryffin puts a round in his neck. 'Just you and me. Still fancy your odds?'

'Might have to even them a little.' Gryffin hears the roof panel come free of its supports but doesn't move out of the way fast enough. It slams him face down into the ground. Gryffin grunts as he pushes to his knees, shoving the panel off his back as he straightens. Thick black smoke fills the air, cutting the visibility down to barely a few feet ahead of him. Alarms shriek and block out any other sounds from the ship. Gryffin lets the control implant out, hoping it will help him see where the hell he's going.

He's going to kill Sayber. That one thought goes round and round in his head as he picks his way through the carnage. 'Sayber! Where the fuck are you!'

He ducks and a round strikes the wall above his head. 'This would be easier on both of us if you'd just lie down and die.'

'Just thinking the same thing.' Gryffin scans the command deck but he might as well be blind.

Through the alarms, he hears a faint creak of a footstep behind him. He spins around, the knife already in his hand. It digs into flesh and he pulls down. Sayber shrieks in pain and tries to fight him off. Sayber's knife slashes at his chest but ricochets off his implant instead of skin. Gryffin pulls his knife free and lashes out again.

Sayber's arm hangs limply by his side, blood pouring freely from the large wound that stretches from his shoulder to his hand. He smiles at Gryffin and holds his knife out in front of him. 'I didn't want it to come to this, Gryffin. You know that, right?'

'You want *Ares* so bad you'd destroy her?'

'I want the ship but if it means taking her down to take you down, it's worth it.'

'So you want the Nomad?'

'No. I want your head removed from your body. No point just injuring you and hoping you'll see sense and fuck off. You'll just go back to Aleena like you always do. Let her kiss it better.'

'What the hell do you mean by that?'

'Oh come on, Gryffin. I know you two have been sleeping together.'

'What?'

'I saw you, okay!'

'When?'

'Months ago. We brought supplies to Ultar. You and

Aleena got deep into some negotiations by all accounts. I came looking for you and what did I see? Just you and her having a romantic goodbye at her door. She even kissed you. So, tell me, Captain. Why is it okay for you to have someone but when I ask you to save someone I care about you can't be bothered, huh? Why is that, cause it doesn't seem a damn bit fair to me.'

'Milara One.'

'Oh, so you do remember.'

'You had someone on the station?'

'Of course I did. I'd only seen her a few times but I cared about her. She was important to me. Not to you though. She died in that attack. Why couldn't you give the order to help? If I'd told you the truth would you have gone to help? Would you have done anything differently?'

'No.'

'I didn't think so. That's your problem though, isn't it. There's not enough humanity left in you. You can't see beyond your personal needs. To hell with anyone else on the ship.'

'I lost control. Aleena chained me up. Stayed with me so I wouldn't hurt anyone.'

'Give me a fucking break.'

'I'm damned if I'm letting you take *Ares*.'

Sayber laughs. 'You don't have a choice.' He hits a control on his wrist unit and Gryffin's ocular implant shuts down. 'Should be careful who you let work on your implants.'

Gryffin blinks to try and clear his vision, but he's screwed. Without the ocular implant he's left with his human eyes which are pretty much useless. Everywhere he looks, there a thick black fog clouding the image. Thanks to the emergency lights flickering everywhere he turns, he can't even make out basic shapes around him. 'Sayber!'

'Problem, sir?'

Gryffin turns in the direction the voice came from, but the lights are messing up the little he can see.

'Sorry, sir. You want me to stand still?'

His voice comes from the opposite direction. Sayber's just fucking with him now. Something creaks behind him, but the bastard strikes before Gryffin turns. He slams something heavy between Gryffin's shoulder blades, driving him to the ground. Sayber repeats the attack and pain explodes through his body. He ducks to the side and rams his metal fist where he hopes Sayber is. It connects and Sayber howls in pain. Gryffin grunts as Sayber punches him straight in the ocular implant. The impact vibrates deep inside his head. It feels like the screws attaching it to his face have been shoved further in. Warm blood trickles into his eye, messing up what little vision he has left.

Sayber fixes a restraint around Gryffin's flesh wrist as he's trying to convince his head to stop spinning. He hears metal scraping across the floor so turns to the side, narrowly missing a third strike from Sayber. Sayber swings the pipe at him again, driving it into Gryffin's side. Gryffin tries to get up, but Sayber has locked the other end of the restraint to something. He twists to the side and kicks out behind him. Sayber crashes to the ground, landing hard. Gryffin slams his boot back, getting Sayber in the leg. Sayber screams and punches where his flesh locks with his prosthetic arm. The spear of pain rams into his sensitive connectors.

He shoves Sayber away but Sayber injects something into his leg. Whatever it was, it hits him like another blow from Sayber. His body grows cold and movement becomes a distant memory. He tries to force his body to obey, but the drug has a firm hold.

Sayber straddles Gryffin's chest and digs his knees into his bruised sides as he disarms him. He hears him take a few deep breaths before he speaks again. 'Sorry about that. Not quite a fair fight, but nothing is with you, is it? Had to tip the scales in my favour.' The blade digs into the centre of his neck, forcing his head up. Sayber leans closer and warm blood trickles from the wound as it cuts deeper into his skin.

'In case you hadn't guessed, I'm relieving you of your command.' The knife moves away from his neck as Sayber repositions it. Adrenaline or the drug or a mix of both helps to dull the pain as Sayber digs the knife in and pulls it across Gryffin's neck.

24

Kellyn kicks at the ceiling panel desperate to get into the command deck. Through the steel mesh, he watched the fight between Sayber and Gryffin, helpless to do anything about it. They're trying to break into the command deck but it's taking time. Kellyn stops as Sayber takes his knife out and slices it across Gryffin's throat. Kellyn shouts and kicks at the panel again. With a final bone-jarring attack, it gives way, dropping on to the floor inches from Gryffin's head. He leans down and fires at Sayber but just misses the bastard.

Kellyn drops to the ground followed by eight

Nomad. He gestures to the team. 'Get Sayber.' He looks at the group of Nomad with him and spots Desyl. The Nomad has natural piloting skills. It's part of the reason he was brought into the group a few years ago. 'Desyl, I'll need you to help. Get this ship operational and contact the med bay. We need Ryder here now!'

Kellyn crouches down beside Gryffin. His eyes are closed and his breathing erratic. Desyl throws the med kit to Kellyn who stares at the contents. 'This will do damn all. How far are we from anywhere with help?'

Desyl checks the screen and curses to himself. He disappears behind the nav unit, readjusts a few cables and checks again. 'C'mon old girl. We need you.' He hits a few controls and slams his hand against the unit as *Ares'* engines whine into life. 'I'll have us at Ultar in twenty minutes. Nothing else is close to our location. It'll burn the engines out but reckon that's the least of our problems. Ryder is out. Took a blow to the head when the attack started. He's alive but no good to the captain.'

'Fucking perfect. Guess I'm the medic.' Kellyn tears the packaging off a roll of bandage and a pile of gauzes. Gryffin's eyes open as Kellyn presses a bandage to his neck. 'You with us, sir?'

'Sayber...' His voice is barely audible. Shame the same can't be said for the rattle accompanying each shallow breath.

'There's a team after him. Can you hold this in place?'

'Gave me... something.'

Kellyn frowns and then spots the pressure dart a few feet from Gryffin. 'Fair fight I see. Don't worry, sir. We'll get you sorted. I'll try to… hell, this won't stem it for long but it's better than nothing. We're heading to Ultar. This isn't too deep. Nasty though.'

He tapes the bandages in place, then examines Gryffin's eyepiece. 'Shit. This is a mess. Presume your eyesight's gone?'

'Sayber… before…'

'Before what? Before the attack? Hang on – are you saying he messed with your ocular implant?'

'Yeah. Find him.'

'Oh don't you be worrying about that, sir. We'll find him. Desyl. Any sign of Sayber?'

'He's gone. Took an escape pod. He was alone.'

'Fucking brilliant. Right, lock down this ship. I want everything non-essential shut off and all remaining power transferred to the engines. All crew to lock down in their quarters. I don't want anyone wandering around until we know who we can trust.'

Gryffin takes a shaky breath which ends in a gargled cough. Blood bubbles out of his mouth and soaks through the bandage around his neck. He's barely hanging on to consciousness and he's doing a fine job of camouflaging with the metal floor under him. They're losing him.

Kellyn pulls the monitoring kit from beside Gryffin's chair and opens the case. 'Desyl, ship status.' He inserts the fine probe into Gryffin's ocular implant, taking two attempts thanks to his trembling hands.

Once in place, he slices Gryffin's t-shirt open and fits the larger one into a port on his chest and waits as the data loads.

'We've got one engine left,' Desyl reports. 'Heavy damage to levels three and four. Life support failed in those areas. System overloads reported throughout the ship, but can't get a handle on that right now. Just need to keep her heading in the right direction.'

Kellyn checks Gryffin's readings and grimaces. 'Sir, I don't know if you can hear me. Your implants are trying to support you, but the drug is messing with them. I can't get your eyesight back yet. There's too much damage to the implant. It'll need a fair bit of work first. The knife damaged your windpipe and vocal cords. The implants on your lungs are getting oxygen around your body but it's not steady. Not sure how long you'll stay conscious.'

Blood dribbles out of Gryffin's mouth as he coughs. 'Sayber...my...kill.'

'You've just had your throat sliced. With all due respect, sir, shut the fuck up.'

Gryffin closes his eyes and takes another unhealthy sounding breath.

Kellyn gets up and joins Desyl at the nav station. 'We're going to lose him unless we get him help ASAP. His implants can only do so much. It could go either way. Contact Aleena and give her the heads up. We'll need personnel and medical supplies as well as a secure location on the surface to treat the injured. Tell her about the captain too. I'll need her to help stitch him back together. After that tell Rayde that Sayber attempted mutiny. Gryffin is alive but injured. We're on the way to Ultar and will update him once we know more. Get in touch with the rest of the crew. Tell them to prepare for a potentially bumpy landing.'

'I can't believe Sayber tried this. What the hell was he thinking?'

'Don't care to be honest. He betrayed the captain. Betrayed the Nomad. He's just signed his death notice. If the captain gets through this, round two will go very differently.'

25

Aleena kicks her old mare, encouraging the horse to pick up the pace as she directs her towards the lake. All around her Ultarans move through the trees on horse, foot, or by cart. Like her, each one is carrying blankets, medical supplies, or water. Back at the town hall, another team is setting up a medical suite which should be able to deal with numerous casualties.

She never expected to get a distress call from *Ares*. The message from Desyl was painfully brief. *Ares* is severely damaged, they have suffered losses, and have substantial casualties - Gryffin included. Her heart is aching for the Nomad. In the year or so they have been trading, she has grown close to the crew and it saddens her to hear some have lost their lives.

Then she hears it. *Ares* is coming... but something is wrong. The sound is different. Almost painful to listen to. She reins in her horse and scans the night sky. One of the women points to the west. She follows her lead and gasps when she sees the vessel in the distance. Or rather, sees the red glow from her engines, followed by a dark plume of smoke. 'The lake. They will hit the lake.'

As they rush through the trees, the whine from *Ares* increases. With an explosion of metal impacting water the vessel crashes and comes to a stop at the far side of the lake with her bow buried in the bank. She knows she should move towards the ship, but like her horse, she is frozen to the spot. Her horse makes the decision for her and follows the other Ultarans through the trees to the lake. Aleena dismounts and hands the reins to one of her people. She take a few steps closer to the edge of the water and jumps as an explosion sounds from inside the vessel.

The main bulk of the vessel is underwater with only the top few decks above the surface. She has no idea what to do. Until someone inside opens a hatch, they have no access to the ship. What if there is no one conscious to open the ship? Perhaps there is no one left.

Finally, a lone figure appears from the side of the ship and climbs down a ladder embedded in the hull. 'Bring a boat.' She climbs into the rowboat with three of her people and places a med kit on the floor in front of her. The hulking form of *Ares* seems all the more intimidating the closer they get to her.

The dark-haired man smiles as she nears. She recognises him but does not believe they have ever been introduced.

'Aleena, I'm Desyl.'

'What happened?'

'Mutiny.'

Aleena does not immediately register what he said. 'Mutiny? Who?'

'Sayber.'

'Where is he now?'

Desyl shakes his head. 'Gone. Took an escape pod and disappeared. Listen, we need serious help. Problem is, the ship is in lockdown and Sayber disabled some of the systems. It's like a death trap in there. We have a lot of injured Nomad but until we clear them, we don't know who else was working with Sayber. Can you send over some extra med kits? There's a handful of Nomad we know for sure wouldn't betray the captain. They can start going from room to room, treating and clearing crew.'

'Of course. I can also send some people over to help. Can you open the cargo bay?'

'We're working on it.'

A hatch further along the side of the ship opens and a Nomad leans out. 'Got access to the main crew quarters, sir.'

'Great. Aleena, if you could get some people over

and start seeing to the injured.'

'Of course.' She turns to the others in the boat. 'I will remain on *Ares*. Organise the teams. Make sure everything is in place.'

Desyl holds out his hand to her. 'I'll take the bag. You climb. It's a long one. You sure you're okay to do this?'

Instead of answering, and possibly talking herself out of it, she passes him the bag and accepts his help to board *Ares*. She looks up the length of the ladder but cannot see the top of the ship. Desyl disappears into the darkness above her and she takes a deep breath then begins the long climb.

When she finally reaches the top she must refrain from kissing the deck. She only hopes she does not have to go back the same way. Resisting the urge to peer over the side, she follows Desyl to a hatch in the centre of the deck. Aleena stares up at the massive sails towering above her. She had never seen the ship from this perspective before. She is truly breath-taking.

Desyl disappears down the hatch and waits underneath to catch her as she slides in. She takes the torch from Desyl and follows him along the narrow and incredibly cramped access tunnel. She climbs down three floors and carries on along an equally narrow corridor before she is finally lowered into the command deck. This is her first time here and it will certainly stay in her memory. Among the destroyed units, strobe lights, and wails from machinery is blood - a lot of blood.

Aleena turns around and gasps when she sees Gryffin lying at the side of the upper platform. Kellyn is crouched beside him, checking a small monitor.

She approaches Gryffin and her hand flies up to her mouth. There is blood on the bandage around his neck and smeared on his chest. 'What happened?'

'Sayber tried to kill him,' Kellyn explains as he keeps pressure on Gryffin's neck. 'We got here just in time. Bastard slit his throat. Didn't go all the way through, but it won't stop bleeding.'

'Why is he restrained. Is he-'

'No. Sayber did it. Can't unlock him yet. He's got the code. It'll take time to cut them off. He programmed the ocular implant to fail then shot him up with some sort of drug. Don't know what, but the captain can't move. Not much chance of losing the fight if your opponent can't see or move.'

'How honourable of him.'

Gryffin's eyes open briefly and he winces. 'Aleena?'

She can barely hear his words. 'Please do not speak, Captain. For once could you not have come to Ultar for an uneventful visit?'

He smiles slightly. 'Boring.'

She wipes his hair off his face, careful not to brush against the damaged implant around his eye. She looks away from it. Some of the screws have come loose, exposing the deep holes in his flesh. Somehow, she forces a smile on her face. 'There is nothing wrong with boring. Can I examine the wound?'

He closes his eyes, which she takes as a yes. Moving

slowly and carefully, she peels the tape back and lifts the bandage from the wound. 'That will need a lot of stitches.'

'That's why we need your kit. Med bay is shut off.'

'You are not suggesting we treat him here? He needs to be brought to the town hall. We have everything we need there.'

'We can't move him, Aleena.' Kellyn points to the heavy restraint around Gryffin's wrist. 'These were designed to hold him. That's why Sayber used them. Until we can unlock them or cut the metal railing he's stuck here.'

'This is more than I can manage. He is seriously injured and needs to be in a med bay. He needs a surgeon – not me.'

'Yeah, well it's all we've got. To be honest, we're happier about that. We don't know who to trust right now, Aleena. Sayber and his men mixed with your people too. It won't take much to finish Gryffin off. We can't give him or anyone else that chance. He's only got the two of us to patch him up.'

She nods, understanding the situation. She pulls on a pair of gloves even though the chance of avoiding infection has long passed. Gryffin's eyes are closed, his breath coming in short, shallow gasps. Fear of further complicating the wound and potentially jeopardising his life is giving her reason to pause. 'I do not believe I am the right person to help him. I have only sutured minor wounds in the past.'

Kellyn attempts a smile but it turns onto a grimace.

'Just think of it as a series of smaller wounds.' He places a hand on her arm. 'He needs you to do this. We need you to do this. Ryder is on his way to your facility. Knocked unconscious. You're it.'

She nods weakly and begins to clean the wound as Kellyn gets up to join Desyl. 'Anything showing up?'

Desyl shakes his head. 'Nope. Doesn't mean the bastard's not out there. Who knows what he did to the sensors.'

'Check the systems you can.' Kellyn joins Aleena on the floor again and pulls on a pair of gloves before he prepares the suture packs she'll need.

Aleena tries to block out everything around her as she deals with the damage caused by Sayber's blade. The cut is extensive but straight and the edges are clean. It is Gryffin's condition which concerns her more. His breathing is irregular and occasionally stops entirely for too long before beginning again. Eventually, she places the last stitch and sits back on her heels, exhausted. 'That is all I can do for him here.'

Kellyn cleans the blood from Gryffin's neck and dresses it. 'You did good, Aleena. He'll owe you for this.'

'He can repay me by waking up.'

'I second that.'

She leans back against Gryffin's command chair and takes a deep breath. That was something she never wishes to do again. Just as she allows herself to relax a little, the unit connected to Gryffin's chest shrieks loudly. Kellyn grabs it and checks the readings. 'Fuck it! His heart has stopped.'

Aleena immediately leans over to help but Kellyn shakes his head. 'The implant on his heart has stopped. We need to get that working, not his actual heart. In the locker by his chair. I need the green box. Desyl. Get over here!'

She finds what he needs and opens the lid. Aleena stares in horror at the two needles inside. Before she can comment Kellyn takes the box from her and carefully removes one of the needles. 'Desyl, watch his stats. Tell me when I'm in.'

Kellyn leans over Gryffin's prone body and feels along the plating on his chest implant. 'C'mon where are you? Got it!' He guides the tip of the needle into a port on the large implant and pushes it into Gryffin's body.

'It's hooked in,' Desyl says.

Kellyn takes the second needle and repeats the procedure a little further down Gryffin's chest implant. As soon as it is in place Kellyn types in some commands and the two Nomad stare at the screen. Aleena is afraid to ask what they are doing. All she knows is that they are trying to restart Gryffin's heart. That is far more important than her questions.

After a long wait, the men smile and visibly relax. 'That's it, Captain.' Kellyn slumps back against the chair next to Aleena. 'His heart is going again.'

'His heart or the implant on his heart?'

'His heart,' Desyl says. 'The implant that would usually control it is struggling after whatever Sayber gave him. It'll take time to reset itself.' He nods to the green box beside them. 'That's controlling his heart until the implant is sorted.'

She looks down at the plain metal box with chipped green paint. 'That is the only thing keeping him alive?'

Kellyn nods. 'Short term.' He gets up and looks around the wreckage of the command deck. 'We'll get the corridor cleared so we can access the cargo hold. There are tools down there we can use to cut the restraints off. He's just going to have to stay where he is for a little bit.'

Aleena removes the blood-stained gloves and drops them into the top of the used medical kit. Gryffin's breathing has not improved. She knows his implants assist with that, but she is unsure how or even if they will be able to help him in this situation. She checks the green box and sees the steady beat of his heart displayed on the screen.

Using a surgical glove, she picks up the dart. She had never trusted Sayber. After their first encounter he had made his feelings towards her perfectly clear. But never did she think he would do something like this. Drugging and restraining Gryffin so he could kill him? It is a dirty trick. She takes Gryffin's cold hand in hers and squeezes, hoping for some reaction. Instead of pulling away and shouting at her, nothing happens. 'Kellyn?'

The Nomad moves away from the doorway and crouches down in front of her. 'He okay?'

'Yes. I have a proposal for you. As you said, some of

my people spoke to Sayber. I do not believe any Ultarans would be involved, but until we know for sure, perhaps it would be best to move Gryffin to my house. I can ensure he will be well looked after and you may post trustworthy Nomad there. It may be easier to limit comings and goings.'

'You sure about that? He's a grumpy git when he wants to be. Won't be an easy job - believe me.'

She smiles and nods. 'I fully believe you. I am more than up for the challenge.'

'If you're sure, that'll be perfect. I know Desyl and the team with me are clear. We'll take turns to guard your place. Once I'm sure all traitors are dealt with we can get *Ares* back to her old self and save you from the captain. I'll do that as fast as I can - get him out of your hair before you get the urge to kill him yourself,' he adds with a wink.

26

Gryffin wakes with a start as the side of his bed dips slightly. He opens his eyes and relaxes when he sees Aleena sitting beside him. 'Apologies for startling you, Captain. How do you feel?'

He tries to swallow but it feels like he's got razor blades wedged in his throat. 'Where am I?'

'In my house. What do you remember?'

'Last thing is you checking the wound.' He touches his neck but can't feel the stitches through the heavy padding. 'You fix me?'

'With Kellyn's assistance. We had the great pleasure of stitching your neck together again. Can you see?'

'Yeah. The implant okay?'

'Kellyn and Desyl were able to repair the damage and remove the…' she looks away for a moment. 'How did they phrase it? Ah yes, they removed the additional programming Sayber added during your last check. Does that make sense?'

'Yeah.'

'Well, Kellyn activated your ocular device this morning and your readings appear to be as they should. There is no lasting damage.' She smiles but it's forced.

'You okay?'

'Me? I am fine. Relieved you are awake. I was worried. You have been unconscious for nearly three days. We still do not know what Sayber gave you. Whatever it was, it took your implants some time to neutralise it.'

He lifts his arm to see the restraints are gone. 'How'd I get here?'

'Your men were able to open most of the internal doors and clear a path to take you down. I decided it would be better for you to recover here. You did not answer my question. How do you feel?'

'Fine.'

She smiles softly and shakes her head. 'I would imagine fine is far from how you feel. You were incredibly lucky. We were able to repair the damage the incision caused. Apart from some slight damage to your vocal cords, you will live to fight another day.'

'Who's in command?'

'Kellyn for the moment. Rayde has appointed one of his own crew to replace Sayber. A man called Klay, I believe. He will step in when he arrives. Kellyn and Ryder are downstairs for protection while Desyl is on *Ares* overseeing repairs. It seems Sayber has not made an appearance yet. Perhaps he has left the area.'

Gryffin grunts, instantly regretting it as the razors dig deeper into this throat. He winces and lies back in bed. He seriously messed up and nearly lost his head as a result. He's the captain of *Ares*. He should have seen what Sayber was planning.

'He seemed trustworthy to me also,' Aleena says, reading his thoughts.

'Can you stop doing that?'

'Stop doing what?'

'Getting in my head.'

'I apologise. I have some soup on the burner for you.' When Aleena leaves him alone, he pushes the covers aside, relieved to see he's still wearing boxers. It takes a few attempts but he finally gets to his feet, pausing as the room flips on its head a few times. He reaches up to touch the bandage circling his neck. Every breath, every swallow sends shards of glass past the wound. His holster and gun are sitting on the dressing table on the far side of the room. There's no sign of his uniform. Knowing Aleena she's either washing the blood off it or it's been thrown away.

Gryffin slowly crosses the room and leans on the dressing table, one hand to either side of his gun as he catches his breath. Having a ceiling panel land on him has left an impressive bruise on his chest and back if the pain is anything to go by.

Gryffin closes his eyes and lowers his head, ignoring the throbbing along the wound on his neck. He knows his eyes are purple but he couldn't care less. He's furious - at Sayber... and himself. He failed the Nomad. Failed to see one of their own was planning something like this. Failed to stop it dead before it risked even one Nomad life. Each injury. Each drop of Nomad blood spilt by Sayber. Each life lost... it's on him. Every decision he made since taking command of *Ares* led them to here and now. Would Rayde have gone to that station to rescue Sayber's woman? Not a chance in hell. Rayde would never have pulled off course for something like that.

He opens his eyes and looks at the pale, bruised face staring back at him. Would Sayber have accepted that decision from Rayde? Probably. In all his years on *Ares*, he can't remember anyone questioning Rayde - apart from Creed. The fact he even suggested something is going on between himself and Aleena is ridiculous. Sayber had been on board long enough to know Gryffin isn't like that. The Nomad and the ship come first.

He'd turned down chances to be with women over the years. Sayber knew that. Hell, he'd never even been with a damn woman. The scarring the Scientist left on his groin would raise too many questions. Any answer he came up with would ensure he spent the evening alone. Easier all round if he avoided those situations.

His hand rests on his gun on the dressing table. He's pretty damn sure Sayber wouldn't have tried this with Rayde. This is down to him and him alone. If even one member of the crew didn't respect him enough to join with Sayber, that's his fault. Sayber just gave the crew an out. Some way of getting their ship back from him. What makes him so different to Rayde? Apart from trading, he's stuck to Rayde's way of doing things. If he believes the rumours, he's feared more than Rayde was. Fear isn't something he wants from his crew. Never did.

His eyes move down to the metal screwed to his chest. Did Sayber do this because of what he is? Because he's not a real person? Not a real captain? Not a real threat? That's the only difference as far as he can tell. Rayde is human and he's... he doesn't know what he is. A cyborg. A machine. An experiment. A mistake. Using what he is helped bring strength to the Nomad. They had food and weapons. Their ships needed fewer repairs.

So why the hell did a dozen or more Nomad decide Sayber was a better fit than him? Whatever the reason, he'll go down in Nomad history as the first captain to deal with a mutiny. What a fucking brilliant way to start his command. Disgracing Rayde and the Nomad in one go. How the hell does he come back from this? How can he stand in front of his crew with the scar across his neck as a constant reminder of his fuck-up?

He slumps forward, his metal hand leaving an

impression on the wood as he hangs on. His legs tremble, struggling to hold him upright as the enormity of what happened settles on top of him, adding its crippling weight to everything else he's carrying around with him. Non-stop constant fucking reminders of every mistake, every error in judgement. It all started when he was a child and he stepped on the transport with the other children. He doesn't remember much else from his life before the Scientist got him, but he remembers that. Remembers the excitement, then the terror, then the pain.

Before he realises what he's doing, his gun is out of its holster and pressed against his ocular implant. One bullet and he'd reset everything. Put things right. He should have died with the others. He was meant to die. No one should have survived to remember that place.

He clicks the safety off and closes his eyes. The sleek curve of the trigger presses against the pad of his finger. He's lost track of the number of times he's fired this gun. Never ones has he faltered - except when it's pointed at his own head.

Gryffin curses and slips the safety back on before slamming the gun onto the dressing table. He glares at the scratched surface of the weapon like it's doing this to him on purpose. It's got nothing to do with the weapon – damn knows he's tried a variety.

Something stops him every single time. It's like a block is thrown up between his brain and the commands to his hand. There's something inside him, some program, or implant. Some sort of artificial wall that steps in, stopping him. Every. Damn. Time. The machine in him isn't ready to die.

'Gryffin.'

His eyes shoot open and he looks up to find Aleena standing in the doorway. A solid wooden tray is in her hands with a bowl of soup and some of the cheese bread she's known for. His hand is still on his gun. Any hope she didn't see his display disappears as soon as he meets her eyes. She's crying.

Aleena places the tray on the end of the bed and faces him, her hands clasped together. She looks at the gun, still under his hand, then at the deep grooves his fingers left in the wood. He's never been an expert at reading emotions but he doesn't have to be to see the shock on her face.

He could slice through the awkward silence that follows her arrival. The only thing he can do is pretend it didn't happen. 'Thanks for the food.'

She frowns at the tray on the bed as if she had forgotten all about it. She rests a hand on the edge of the tray straightening it on the covers before clasping her hands in front of her again. '*Kratos*... it has just landed. Rayde will be here shortly. Ryder left a new uniform in the cupboard for you.'

He lifts his hand off the gun, hoping she doesn't go there with him. 'Thank you.'

'Gryffin...'

He turns around to look at her. 'Thank you, Aleena.'

As she disappears downstairs he releases the breath he was holding. He was hoping he'd get another few days before Rayde arrived. He doesn't have the energy to fight for his position. Not his decision. Pulling open the wardrobe he looks at the neat pile of black clothes. Resigned to the impending ass-kicking, he pulls the clothes out and staggers over to the bed. He dumps his boots on the ground then slowly and painfully gets dressed, pausing for a rest after his trousers and t-shirt. Once he's grappled with his boots he's exhausted. He should have designed a uniform that was easier to put on.

Gryffin pushes to his feet and makes it back over to the table to retrieve his holster. Aleena knocks on the door. 'I thought I heard some banging. Are you all right?'

She probably thought he'd finished what he started earlier. 'I'm fine.'

'You look as though you are going to collapse. Can I assist at all?'

He wants to send her away, but the words don't come out fast enough. She takes the holster from him. 'Lift your arms, please.'

She buckles it around his waist and crouches down to fit the straps around his leg. He passes her the smaller holster for his other leg and leans heavily on the table as she straps it on. 'You are not strong enough for this meeting. You can barely stand.'

'It won't take long.'

Aleena takes the metal knee pads off the bed and lowers to the floor in front of him again. 'Is this the correct way?'

'Other way.' She turns it around and fits the straps in place. 'I am amazed you and your crew can walk with all this strapped to you. It is surprisingly heavy.' She stands up and examines him. 'All done.'

'Thank you.' He carefully lowers onto the bed, making sure not to knock over the tray of food. Gryffin takes the cuff from the bedside table and fastens it around his wrist where it's been since she made it for him. 'I do appreciate everything you're doing.'

Aleena's nod is quick and not followed by any of her usual chatter. 'Should I offer him some food? I am not sure what your customs are.'

'No food. He'll say his piece then leave. I'll meet him outside.'

'You will do no such thing. You will stay where you are and eat something before he arrives. We put quite a bit of effort into keeping you alive. I would greatly appreciate if you did not act foolishly and undo that. I assure you, I would be... deeply upset if anything were to happen to you. Do you hear me, Captain?'

Without waiting for a response, she slips out the door, closing it loudly behind her again.

27

Aleena stands at the sink in her small but comfortable kitchen, staring out at nothing in particular. The clouds had gathered about an hour ago, bringing heavy rainfall that danced across the metal roof outside her back door. She wants to believe she imagined what she saw when she entered Gryffin's room, but she knows that is not the case.

When she reached the top of the stairs and saw him with his weapon to his head, time had stopped. Her feet had refused to obey her from that moment on. Fear, shock, helplessness, to name a few, had taken over. Had he chosen to... there was nothing she could have done. No way she could have... what exactly? Rushed in and pulled the gun from his hand? Gryffin would have died and she would have been utterly helpless to do anything but watch.

Since that one day months ago when they were forced to lock him in a cage in the old mine, she began to understand the Nomad captain. Although he had not spoken of it again, the few details he parted with had left her cold and more than a little unsettled. Perhaps it was stupidity or naivety on her part, but not for one minute did she contemplate how he felt about everything. She knew what he had experienced was truly horrific. She knew the modifications caused him great pain. Did she truly believe that was the extent of his trauma? Was she that absorbed in her own life, in his protection of their world, that she failed to see what was going on?

Or did she not allow herself to see. Perhaps that is it. Perhaps, knowing she would be powerless to comprehend, to help him in any way, she had chosen to ignore the issue.

That thought unsettles her greatly. If that is the case, she is ashamed of herself and her actions. Her parting words with him had come from the heart. She cares about him. Not romantically, but deeply. His actions when he first arrived on Ultar forever tarnished him. The lives of the Ultarans he took were always with him, following behind him like a shadow. She could not unsee those deaths. But as hard as she tried otherwise, he had become a friend. A truly unconventional, erratic and volatile friend, but one nonetheless. She imagines her feelings to be that of a sister for a brother - her being the older more sensible sibling of course. Coming so close to losing him as she had is terrifying.

Another ugly thought enters her mind. Had he tried to take his life before? Were his actions driven by his past or by Sayber's mutiny? Perhaps a combination of the two. If he leaves on *Ares*, could it be the last time she sees him? Their line of work made that a possibility, but now after nearly losing him, she's loathe to see him step on to his ship to deal with his problems alone.

A sharp knock on her front door startles her out of her thoughts. She wipes her eyes with her sleeve as she opens the door. A tall, broad man stands on her doorstep. His thick auburn hair is tied in a long ponytail as is his wiry beard. Dark eyes peer at her from under a heavy brow. Her eyes move from his face to the blade hanging from his belt. His calloused hand is resting on the hilt, his thumb rubbing against the worn leather strap wrapped around the handle. 'Aleena?'

His deep voice is commanding, cold, and completes the initial impression of the man - she does not like him. 'Rayde I presume.'

'You got Gryffin here?'

There is no explanation for how she feels, but she does not want this man in her house. In truth, she does not want him anywhere near Gryffin. She peers around him, relieved to see Kellyn standing to the side of the door. He frowns at her then smiles and nods. Forcing a courteous smile on her face she steps aside. 'He is upstairs - first door on the left. High Commander, he is still very weak. I am sure you appreciate rest is vital to his recovery. I trust you will not keep him long.'

Rayde's brows drop lower, nearly covering his eyes. 'Excuse me?'

'I only have Gryffin's best interests at heart.'

'We are grateful for your actions but we are his family. We will see to his recovery. I suggest you stay the hell out of my way.' Rayde pushes past her, dwarfing her narrow staircase with his broad frame. Needing to get some fresh air, she steps outside and leans against the wall, not caring that the rain is still falling.

'You okay?'

She nods at Kellyn. 'I do not like that man.'

Kellyn laughs. 'Not many do. Haven't seen anyone stand up to him like that before, well, not since Gryffin announced he was trading. You're a tough one.'

'Rayde is jeopardising Gryffin's well-being by removing him from our care.'

'I get that. His rule through. If he wants Gryffin on *Ares*, Gryffin will go. That's the way it works. Hey, if it helps, we'll all be keeping an eye on him. You look pale. You sure you're okay?'

'Thank you for your concern, Kellyn. I am well. It has been an emotional few days.'

He leans against the wall with her, looking out at the lights from *Ares* in the distance. 'We owe you a hell of a lot, you know that, right?'

'There is no need-'

'Yes, there is.' He pushes his wet, blond hair from his face. 'We need Gryffin. The Nomad need him.' He looks over his shoulder and lowers his voice. 'Rayde was good, don't get me wrong. But the way he did things... it didn't put food on our plates. And when it did, it was taken from others who needed it.' He holds up his hands as Aleena looks at him. 'I know, I know, we tried the same stunt on Ultar, but if you hadn't fought for a deal the way you did, we'd still be following that path.' He laughs harshly. 'We'd be dead. Thanks to you and whatever the hell you said to Gryffin, the Nomad are finally a group I'm proud to be a part of. Thank you.'

She squeezes his arm as she leans against him. 'You do not know how much I needed to hear that right now.' Aleena closes her eyes, listening to the rain as she leans against Kellyn's arm, taking the support he's offering. His words have comforted her a little, but she knows seeing her friend as she had today will never leave her memory.

28

Gryffin stands to attention as Rayde steps into the room.

'Sit please, before you fall.'

Rayde lowers onto the chair next to the bed and examines the large bandage around Gryffin's neck. 'Got you good, son. How are you feeling?'

Gryffin swallows painfully a few times. 'Fine.'

Rayde smiles and shakes his head. 'Seems nothing changes. Well, except for your voice. That huskiness won't do you any harm when you're interrogating. Gives your voice more menace.'

Gryffin doesn't reply. He doesn't need anything else

to make him more intimidating - the metal screwed into him does a good enough job. Rayde sits back in the chair and the room falls silent for a few minutes.

'I owe you an apology, son.'

Gryffin looks at Rayde, wondering if he's hearing things.

'Yes, I did just say that,' Rayde says. 'I got a little carried away with your training. I know that. I had - well, still have - my reasons for pushing you so hard. You see when I found you... well, it was one of the most horrific scenes I've ever witnessed. You were so small, so weak and scared. I wanted to give you something else to concentrate on instead of what had happened to you. I thought by pushing you to fight, to stand up for yourself and to be someone to be feared instead of someone living in fear...' he pauses and shakes his head. 'I went too far, son.'

'You didn't.'

Rayde looks up at him. 'What?'

'It all helped me.' He swallows a few more times, trying to convince his voice to do what he wants it to.

'Probably best you rest that voice of yours. So, we're good?'

Gryffin nods. 'Not changing the deals.'

Rayde nods. 'I know. I got that point loud and clear.' He looks around the room. 'Besides, it seems to be working in your favour at the moment. Wouldn't have had this much TLC if you'd stuck to destroying the colony. I'm not saying I fully agree, but I'll keep my mouth shut. So, you ready to go back to your ship?'

Gryffin doesn't reply.

'What Sayber did... shocked the hell out of me too. I didn't see it coming.'

'I should have.'

Rayde sighs loudly as he stretches his legs out in front of him. 'You read minds now too? Believe me, nothing you could have done.'

'Would he have turned on you?'

Rayde pauses then shrugs. 'Maybe. Who knows. Might have taken my head clean off if he did. Again, who the hell knows. Being captain is about making decisions and sticking to them. Consequences be damned. You'll never know how the other path would have turned out. As it stands, the only thing you need to do is get up, walk back to your ship and face your men as their captain. Scars, bruises and all. They need to see that you're unaffected by what happened. Sayber mutinied. You quashed it. Repair the ship and move on.'

Gryffin assumed this meeting was about him being kicked out of the Nomad. He never thought Rayde would let him take *Ares* again. He wants to go back to her, but it would take one impressive act to convince the crew he's unaffected. He can barely stand. He runs a shaky hand through his hair, trying to come up with some excuse that won't tip Rayde the other way.

'She was right.'

'Sir?'

'That Aleena one. She said you were weak. Told me in no uncertain terms I'm not to keep you from your rest.'

'Sir... I-'

Rayde holds up a hand. 'She's looking out for you. I get that, but it's no longer needed. Time to get back to *Ares* and leave this planet. You've been here long enough, Gryffin.'

He nods, but it's the last thing he wants to do. He's not ready to go back. Getting dressed took the last of his energy reserves. He'd be impressed if he could walk down the stairs never mind back to *Ares*.

Rayde gets up and reaches into the pocket of his jacket. 'Picked this up from a station I was just on. Helps to give you a kick - energy-wise.'

Gryffin glances at the syringe in Rayde's hand. 'My implants won't let it in my system.' The truth is he doesn't want it anywhere near his system. He's just recovering from whatever Sayber gave him.

'Stand up. Now!'

Gryffin leans heavily on the bedside table as he stands.

'Walk into the centre of the room.'

He does it, but it's far from the walk of an unaffected captain.

'What part of facing your men as their captain does that pathetic show fall under, huh? If you don't reinforce your command now, you could lose the ship - and not by my orders. It'll be taken out from under you by people who think they're stronger than you, think they have you at a disadvantage. Timing is critical, Gryffin. If you show weakness now, you might as well walk away from that ship and let someone else take command. Now, if you can assure me you'll be able to walk back to *Ares* without landing on your backside, I'll put this away and we won't say any more about it. On the other hand, if there's even the slightest chance you could do something that would give your crew any reason to doubt your... suitability, I suggest you take me up on my offer.'

Gryffin looks down at the syringe in Rayde's hand and nods once.

29

Aleena comes out of the kitchen when she hears heavy footsteps on her staircase - two sets. She curses Rayde under her breath as she stops at the bottom. Rayde smiles triumphantly as he nears. 'Thank you again, Aleena. We are in your debt.' Rayde leaves her house, taking the unsettling feeling with him.

She meets Gryffin with a disapproving shake of her head. 'You are going to kill yourself.'

He looks anywhere but at her. 'I'm fine.'

'You are not fine, Captain,' she hisses, aware that Rayde could still be outside. When he finally looks up, Aleena takes a step back. His eyes are purple. 'Your implants have been activated.'

'We'll get *Ares* repaired and in the air ASAP.'

'I do not care about that. What happened upstairs? Why are your eyes purple? How are you standing? Tell me or you will have to remove me to leave. It may not take much but I will put up a fight.'

'Move.'

She crosses her arms and holds her position. Gryffin takes a step closer trying, as he had many times before, to intimidate her by his size alone. As he steps closer to the light, something catches her attention. There's a red mark on his bicep peeking out from under his sleeve. Aleena pushes the material up and the anger builds deep inside her. She grips his arm, furious at what she sees. 'I do not believe it. He gave you something. What was it? Tell me!'

Gryffin's reaction is swift and brutal. He slams her against the wall, his metal arm braced against her neck. 'Don't touch me.'

Kellyn races into the house but Gryffin points his gun at him, stopping the Nomad in his tracks. 'Sir, we've got to go. Rayde is waiting.'

Aleena stares Gryffin down. 'You could not fasten your holster less than thirty minutes ago. I know he gave you something.' She grips his metal limb in her hands, trying to push him away from her. He glares at her, his purple eyes sending a chill up her spine. His frown lessens a little and he steps back, freeing her. 'This is not right, Gryffin. Stay here, please. You should rest. Your crew can work on repairs while you recover.'

Without a word, he walks away followed by Kellyn who smiles apologetically at her.

Aleena stands at her door and watches Gryffin climb into the transport behind Rayde. As soon as Kellyn boards, the transport disappears down the path back to *Ares*.

Anger still gripping her, she bursts into the guest room and stops dead. On the tray next to the untouched food is an empty syringe. She walks to the window, watching the rain collect on the porch roof. Rayde had successfully managed to use Gryffin to put her back in her place.

ULTAR

A deep rumble wakes Aleena with a start. She sits up in bed and turns on the lamp to check the time. There are still a few hours until dawn. Sleep had evaded her for many hours. The situation with Gryffin and Rayde had kept her mind very much awake until an hour ago.

She hears the rumble again, but this time it does not fade. She swings her legs out of bed and shuffles over to the window, opening it. The cool night air helps convince the remnants of sleep to leave her. She looks towards the trees as the rumbling increases. It takes her longer than it should to realise what it is.

She hurries down the stairs, grabs her coat, and unlocks her front door. The rain quickly soaks her hair, plastering it to her face, but it does not concern her. All her attention is on the light spearing through the darkness as *Kratos* rises above the trees. Aleena shields her eyes as it slowly turns around, momentarily blinding her with its powerful lights. The ship seems to hover for a moment as the rumble increases. The ship accelerates upward, carrying it far from the town in a matter of seconds. She watches with great relief as the lights dim and the ship speeds away from Ultar. Good riddance. Aleena cannot be more relieved to see that back of Rayde.

But then another deep rumble sounds from beyond the trees.

This sound she has come to know over the last few months. Aleena shakes her head. 'Please, no. Do not leave. Not like this.'

Her pleas are drowned out as *Ares* powers up her engines. The immense battleship rises above the trees, a thick dust cloud forming as her engines lift her into the air. *Ares* swings around and her impressive sails slowly rise from the top deck. As the engines power up, the griffin on the back of the ship glares down at her. The engines burn brightly and the roar deepens, sending vibrations through her. With a final growl, the ship accelerates, taking Gryffin away from Ultar.

31

Gryffin collapses back into the less than comfortable chair behind his desk and watches Rayde. The High Commander paces the small room, one hand on the hilt of his blade and the other on his hip. He's upset. Gryffin has known him long enough to know that much. Each time Rayde turns, Gryffin's eyes lock on the blade hanging from his belt. He hates that damn thing. Rayde may not have used it on him since their argument but that doesn't mean Gryffin is going to let his guard down.

He feels worse than he's felt for a long time. Now the drug is wearing off he's finding it difficult to concentrate. Keeping himself upright in the chair is taking all his energy. He's exhausted, hungry, and his throat hurts like hell. Rayde had stopped the transport half a mile from *Ares*, forcing him to walk back on less than steady legs. The drug had given him the strength he needed to get back to the ship but he's paying for it now.

Seeing their Captain storming through the trees a few days after barely evading death had done the trick. Putting a bullet in the heads of the four Nomad Kellyn had identified as working with Sayber had reinforced his position again. The mutiny had failed and everyone involved was dead. All except Sayber. He'd be found sooner or later.

He swallows, sending the knives further down his throat. He looks out the small porthole but Ultar is gone. If Aleena ever lets him set foot on the surface he'd be damn lucky. Attacking her had been bad enough, but leaving in the night like a coward was unacceptable. Not that he had a choice. Rayde wanted *Ares* in the air.

Rayde finally sits and Gryffin relaxes a little. 'I'm worried about you.'

He frowns. That wasn't what he was expecting. 'Why?'

'I've checked your reports and the ship logs. Seems you've been favouring Ultar. We're Nomad, Gryffin. Hint's in the name. You planning on settling there? Getting a nice little house with this leader and making a life for yourself?'

'No, sir.'

'Then what the fuck are you doing? Ultar is a farming colony. Apart from food, it offers nothing. You want to do these... deals or trades, you got to focus on colonies with something to offer! Unless the leader is giving you something you don't want to talk to me about.'

That's twice in the space of as many days that's been brought up. 'No, sir. It's a safe place. We can take time off *Ares*. The men need that.'

'They need it? Is ship life too hard for them, huh? If that's the way they feel kick them off the damn ship and get men who have what it takes.' Rayde leans on the table and it creaks under his weight. 'You and this leader. What's going on?'

'She helps get me in with other colony leaders. They get a lot out of the deals and so do we. There's nothing personal, sir.'

Rayde grunts and sits back. 'I want you to concentrate on other colonies. I know you're the captain but I still have some say in what you do. Send another ship to Ultar if you have to, *Ares* is needed elsewhere. Got it?'

'Yes, sir. I got it.' It comes out brisker than he planned but he's pissed off. He doesn't need Rayde watching his every move.

'You can drop that attitude, son. I'm only looking out for you. We move around for a reason. Ties, familiarities, routine, they can be the downfall of a ship. As it stands, someone wants to get you or *Ares* all they need to do is sit tight on Ultar for a spell and odds are you'll show up. Not exactly making it difficult. And you wouldn't want someone thinking there's something between you and this woman. Might put her in the sights of some unsavoury folk. Final words on that matter.' He gets to his feet and stretches. 'I've got the word out with all the ships. Sayber is at the top of the list. Any reports will be sent directly to you. The kill is yours.'

Gryffin makes to get up, but Rayde stops him. 'You've done your bit in front of the crew. You get yourself to bed before you collapse. Klay has things under control.'

'You made him my second?'

'He's a good Nomad. He'll have your back. I know you had your sights set on Kellyn, but Klay has more time behind him. He'll do you right.'

When the door rattles closed behind him, Gryffin closes his eyes and lies back in the chair. He wants to send Aleena a message to explain his actions, but he has no doubts Rayde will find out and kick his ass.

He'll just have to bide his time. If staying away from Ultar protects Aleena, he'll just have to send other ships to trade in his place... until he figures out another way to bypass Rayde.

With no choice, Gryffin contacts Klay and orders him to set a course for the next colony on the list. *Ares* needs some new parts after the recent crash landing. It would take three days to get there. Plenty of time to get over his injury and get his strength back.

32

The locks on his crate open and Bray squeezes his eyes shut as light pours inside. Bray shuffles up to the far end of the cell and rolls into a ball. He hears voices outside — two belong to guards but the third is a new one. One of the guards leans down to look into the crate. 'Get out.'

Bray doesn't move fast enough for the guard. Before he knows what's happening, he's being dragged out by his ankles. He lands in a heap on the ground and squints in the bright light. He's dragged into a side room used by the guards and thrown in the corner. They unlock his restraints and close the door behind them. He convinces his eyes to open as footsteps approach him. He braces for a beating, but it never materialises. Instead, a plate is placed in front of him and the smell of real food hits him like a physical blow. Not caring who is with him or what might be in the food, his raw need takes over. He shovels the meat and potato into his mouth, stopping a few times when he nearly chokes. Once he's finished every single scrap from the plate, he finally looks up at his companion.

One word instantly hits Bray — kind. It not a word he's used… well not for as long as he can remember anyway. He'd place the man's age anywhere between fifty and sixty. He's clean-shaven with neatly trimmed hair. His nondescript black trousers are immaculate, as is his shirt and long black coat. His soft blue eyes look down at Bray and he swears he sees a hint of sadness.

'Who are you?' Bray winces as the words tear out of his throat.

The man passes him a cup of water. 'Take your time. Sip it.'

Like his eyes, his voice is kind. Whoever he is, he's not from this area of the Sector.

'My name is Hank Avoca. Before I explain more, I need you to confirm something. I'm not saying I don't trust the guards here, but I don't trust the guards here,' he adds with a smile. 'Can you please confirm your name?'

Bray frowns. His first reaction is to tell the man where to go, but he pauses. Nothing about him is suspicious, which in itself is suspicious.

'I promise, I'm here to help you, but I must insist you answer my question first. I'm looking for one particular person. Even with your lack of access to water or any means of grooming yourself, you appear to be the man I'm looking for. I do need confirmation before I continue. Your name, please.'

It had been a long time since anyone had said please to him - especially twice in the space of a few minutes. If talking to this guy kept Bray out of the crate for another few minutes he'd tell him anything he damn well wanted to know. 'Bray.'

'Full name please, Bray. It's important.'

'Brayden Liam Sawyer.'

The man closes his eyes and releases a long breath. He smiles as he kneels to join Bray on the floor. 'I can't tell you how glad I am to have found you, Brayden.' He holds out his hand but Bray flinches away. Hank's smile disappears. 'I am not here to hurt you.'

Bray quietly looks at him. He's not intimidated by this man but that doesn't mean he trusts him.

'I sincerely apologise for what you've been through at this facility. I'm truly horrified by the conditions and treatment you've been subjected to.'

Bray shrugs. 'It's a prison. It's not meant to be fun.'

Hank shakes his head. 'It's not meant to be like this either. I wish there was something I could do to change that, but I cannot.' He shuffles closer to Bray and lowers his voice. 'I don't have much time here, Brayden, and I can't go into details but I need your help.'

Bray leans back against the wall and stretches his legs out. He winces as his joints protest at the new position. After the cramped crate, the freedom rivals the meal he just had. 'I appreciate you getting me out of the crate for a bit but you've got the wrong guy.'

'I assure you I do not. Your brother's name was Daegan.'

A flash of anger rises in Bray. 'What the hell does he have to do with anything?'

'I can't go into details here.'

'So that's it? You expect me to trust whatever you say because you gave me some food and mention my brother?'

'That and the fact I'm going to get you out of here.'

Bray rubs a dirty hand over his face. He frowns when he feels his beard. He must have been in the crate for a few weeks for it to grow so long. 'I'm here until they get bored and kill me. There's no way out.'

Hank smiles sheepishly. 'Not legally, no. But, after what I've seen here today, legal and this facility do not go together. I want to break you out, today.' He glances at the unit on his wrist. 'Well, in ten minutes to be exact.'

Bray stares at the well-dressed man in disbelief. His head is spinning. He has so many questions to ask, but clearly the man is more fond of teasing him with fragmented information than anything substantial. The thought of going back into the crate is enough to have him eager to do anything rather than face that hell again. Escape is impossible though. He's tried often enough. 'You're crazy, you know that. I'm in isolation. Even if I can get out of there, I'm not going to get off this level, let alone the facility. Then there's the small issue of being on a fucking moon.'

Avoca nods slowly. 'I know I'm asking a lot, but I need you to trust me. You'll be taken back to your cell in a few minutes. Once the alarms go off—'

'Alarms?'

'Once the alarms go off,' Hank repeats, 'go to Level 23.'

Bray laughs. 'Hate to break it to you, but the way out is at Level 1.'

'I'm aware of that. As I said, go to Level 23. I'll have the way clear and all doors open for you.'

'How?'

'I know you have a lot of questions, but now isn't the time. Look for a recycling crate with the serial number H-445G. There's a hidden compartment under the main unit.' Hank grimaces. 'I'm afraid it'll be a tight squeeze. I know that's far from ideal after where you've just been.'

Bray opens his mouth to respond, but Hank holds up a hand. 'Time's up.' He gets to his feet and walks over to the door. 'Trust me, Brayden. Do what I said and I'll answer all your questions far away from this place.'

33

'A what?'

'An aide, sir.' Klay rests his hip on the edge of Gryffin's desk. 'Someone to help with reports, to look after you.'

Gryffin raises his eyebrow. 'To what?'

Klay licks his lips as he figures out what to say. 'The aide could vocalise reports for you. Hell, he could write your reports for you. With trading going so well, they could also arrange meetings, look after trading terms. Sir, there's a lot of things you're doing that you don't have to. We're a few hours from a small colony interested in protection. I've been told there are at least seven men in the village who want a shot at joining the crew.'

'How many we need?'

Klay makes a face. 'I was thinking three. Four if you take one for yourself.'

Gryffin leans back in his chair and glares at the pile of reports in front of him. Klay has a point. Keeping track of all the deals was taking most of his time. Not being able to read and having to get all reports vocalised was taking time from his crew too. Time they don't have. Maybe an aide wouldn't be a bad idea. It's a better idea than him learning how to read. Reading took patience - he didn't have a lot of that.

'You want this aide on the crew or just in this role?'

'Just as your aide. Keep things simple. I'm thinking you'd prefer to be on the command deck than behind that desk. Doesn't really suit you.'

'Hate this damn thing. Fine. Final say with me though. I'll be on deck in thirty minutes.'

In less than thirty minutes, he escapes from behind his desk and settles back in his command chair as *Ares* lands on top of a hill a few miles from the village. In stark contrast to Ultar, this planet is barren. The harsh rays from the twin suns have burnt the ground to a rust colour. Trees or any other type of vegetation seems to be in short supply. Leaving Klay in charge of *Ares*, Gryffin meets with the two teams assembled in the cargo hold. They load onto their last functioning transport. Thanks to increased trading they now have the credits needed to fix the other two. Just need to find someone with the parts.

The ramp lowers and, after checking all his implants are covered, Gryffin takes the controls and guides the transport onto the surface. A few minutes later, he lands at the prearranged coordinates and kills the engine.

He steps out and looks around. The intense heat hits him like a blow. Keeping his implants hidden under a black uniform is going to make this an uncomfortable visit. More incentive to get the hell out of there ASAP.

He examines the leader's house, not quite believing what he sees. He's seen better cattle sheds on Ultar. The house seems to be missing half a roof and two windows. The fence surrounding the property consists of a few stakes with a bit of wire strung across them. The garden is bare and littered with broken machinery and rubble.

He looks up as the door opens with a long and ominous creak. Gryffin frowns as the leader makes his way down the gravel path. The man is impossible to age, with a lean build, thinning hair, and too many bones showing through his threadbare shirt.

The leader holds his hand out but Gryffin ignores it. 'You Hal?'

'I am. Thank you for coming. I fear we desperately need your assistance. Aleena said you may be able to help protect us against any further attacks.'

'From who?'

'Slavers. They took what little we had then

destroyed the main water pipe from the well outside town. We don't have the tools to repair it. Bastards took those too.' He looks out to the town and sighs. 'Left us here to die. Seems we weren't worth taking. Not sure to be happy or insulted by that.'

Gryffin turns away from him and walks over to Kellyn. 'Get back to *Ares*. Fill Klay in. We need to keep an eye out for Slavers. Bring back another team to help with the pipe.' Gryffin addresses Hal again. 'This pipe above or below the ground?'

'Above. The ground is too hard to dig in.'

'You got people who can help us repair it?'

'You are going to help us? Not that I am not grateful, but we cannot afford to compensate you.'

'We'll sort that out later. I hear you have men who want to sign up?'

Hal nods. 'Yes. I must admit I am loathed to lose any young-uns, but I will not keep them on a dying colony. How many will you take?'

'I'll decide when I see them. Have them at the ship in an hour.' He gestures over his shoulder at Desyl. 'Show him the pipe. He'll make sure it's fixed. Then we'll sit down and talk.'

Hal opens the door to his house and shows Gryffin to the worn chair in the corner. 'I'll be back in a few minutes. Please make yourself comfortable.'

He hurries off with Desyl in tow, leaving Gryffin and his security alone in the house. After everything the man has endured with the Slaver attack, trust still isn't an issue for him. Then again, after a cursory look around, there's nothing worth stealing.

Thanks to the gaping hole in the roof, there's no escape from the searing heat outside. He wanders into the kitchen area and opens the nearest cupboard. It's empty. As is the next one, and the next. What the hell are these people surviving on? He spots a pile of withered vegetables of some sort on the far counter. Looks nearly as appetising as one of their tasteless ration bars.

The flimsy lock on the back door wouldn't take much convincing to get through. Then again, with some windows missing you wouldn't need to go near the back door to get entry.

Gryffin ducks under the doorway and goes back into the main living area. He's never allowed himself to get personally involved with any of the colonies. Apart from Ultar, he didn't delve into the colony or the leaders in any detail. If Aleena vouched for them that was all he needed. Something about this place is different. It's getting to him. Credits and deals aside, he wants to help.

Damn Aleena. She suggested he come here and now he knows why. Doesn't get her off the hook though. He doesn't appreciate begin played – no matter how worthy the cause. He's going to make a loss on this one. May even have to take credits from his own pocket to deal with it. For the first time that really doesn't bother him.

34

Bray lowers onto the metal bench and stretches his legs out in front of him. As much as he wants to believe Avoca, he's not getting carried away. In all likelihood, he'll be back in the crate by the end of the day. Until then, he's going to stretch his sore, underused muscles for every second of his freedom. He snorts to himself. Freedom. That's something he'll never have again.

He accepted his sentence from the minute it was passed down from the guards. He didn't agree with it but no amount of complaining or feeling sorry for himself would make a damn bit of difference. That didn't mean he was going to lie back and live happily ever after in this place. Every minute of every day was spent trying to find some kink in the system, some chink in the armour that he could squeeze through. So far, his plan had gone disastrously wrong. He must have spent as much time in the crate as he did in his cell. If this Avoca guy can do what he'd failed to do for years, he'd happily hitch a ride. Pride meant nothing when you were locked in a box with your own waste. The only thing he has to lose if this goes wrong is his life and that's not worth much.

He gets to his feet, stretching his arms over his head as he paces the cell. If the man, Hank, is right, the alarms should go off any second. Right on schedule, the alarms scream to life. He hurries over to the bars, unsure of what to expect. An imposing man in a pair of navy overalls approaches his cell and attaches something to the lock. He taps the screen on a handheld unit and the cell opens.

He stares at Bray who remains frozen to the spot. He wasn't expecting someone to come for him. 'You coming or what?'

'Who are you?'

'Heath. I'm a friend of Avoca's. He wasn't sure you'd make it out without help.' His eyes moved from Bray's battered boots, to his ill-fitting filthy uniform before settling on his face. 'No offence but I'm tending to agree. C'mon.'

'Where?'

The guard smiles serenely at him. 'How about a walk in the gardens followed by a swim in the pool?

I'm breaking you out, so can you please move your fucking arse? Avoca won't hang around forever.'

With the decision made, Bray limps out of the cell and him. Heath pauses at the next security door and keys in the code to unlock it. He shoves Bray through and attaches a small box to the panel before he shuts it behind them. 'It's going to blow in thirty seconds.'

Bray turns quickly and forces his battered legs down the stairs. He reaches the next level as the device explodes, propelling debris down the stairs, narrowly missing his head.

Bray clears the next few levels by sheer will alone. His body is screaming for relief after so long in the crate, but it'll have to wait.

He stops at the door to Level 23 and pauses to catch his breath. Or does until Heath grabs him by the front of his shirt and hauls him into the large storage area. Lines of recycling crates and compacters take up the wall to his left and another large unit sits against the right wall. Bray eyes it as he clears the steps down into the room.

Heath notices where his attention is. 'Get a move on. If we're not gone in the next two minutes, we'll be in that incinerator with the other bodies.'

Bray suppresses a shiver and joins him at the last recycling crate towards the back of the room. Heath crouches down and pulls the side off the unit. Bray stares in horror at the tiny compartment under the main body of the box. The crate where he spent the last few weeks is roomy compared to it. He knows it's his only way off this rock, but he can't convince his body to respond.

'What are you waiting for? Get in.'

Bray licks his cracked lips and tries to swallow, but there's no moisture to offer any relief. 'I...'

Heath curses under his breath, then Bray feels something being pressed against his neck. He flinches away, but it's too late. He slumps back into the waiting arms of the guard. 'What was...'

'Just shut up and sleep. You'd better be worth all this hassle.'

Bray opens his mouth to respond but doesn't have the energy. His eyelids grow heavy as whatever he was given works into his system. The last thing he sees is the cramped compartment getting closer as he loses consciousness.

35

An hour later, the transport drops Gryffin back at *Ares*, before turning back to the village. Negotiations with Hal had been quick and uncomplicated. They needed help and were grateful for anything the Nomad could offer. The payment was still to be decided upon, but Gryffin wasn't worried about it. In time, they would settle the debt.

Seven men are at the bottom of the ramp, facing away from the ship. They each stand a little taller when he approaches. Gryffin groans to himself. Recruiting is a necessary part of his job – but easily the part he hates the most. He's not a natural people person. That's part of the reason he leaves the initial colony meetings for Aleena to handle. Unfortunately, if the fleet is to perform as well as he knows they can, he needs to find potential Nomad wherever he can.

He quietly examines the men. Like the leader, they're barely alive. Maybe they see *Ares* as a way of getting off this rock and surviving a little longer.

After leaving them to stew for a few minutes, he finally walks up to the group, starting from one end of the line and working his way along. He doesn't talk to any of them. By looking at them, he knows if they'll fit with the group. As much as the Nomad may need more bodies, from what he's seen, this colony can't afford to lose seven young men. They'll need them here to get things up and running again.

Gryffin stops at the last local, a blond-haired, fresh-faced man a few years younger than him. Unlike the others in the line, this one doesn't look away. He's nervous but looks Gryffin up and down before focusing on the purple lenses over his eyes. 'Name.'

'Chayse, sir.'

'You got family on the surface?'

He shakes his head. 'No, sir.'

'Why the Nomad?'

'I've got nothing left here. I want to be part of something again.' He shrugs. 'I know I don't look like much but I'm strong.'

Gryffin walks away without another word. Attitude and no family to leave behind. Looks like he found his new aide. He joins Klay on the ramp. 'I'll take Chayse.

Third and fifth from the left for the main crew. The others are fit. Look less likely to fall apart if something bumps into them. The colony needs them here.'

'Did the leader sign up?'

Gryffin nods. 'They get hit again they'll be wiped out.'

'Payment?'

'They'll come good. For now, it's one way.'

'What supplies do you want to leave? We don't have a lot to spare.'

'We're due to restock in a week. Leave us enough to get to the next colony. Everything else stays here.'

'We need something in return. I get what you're saying but we start leaving food on colonies we'll earn our fair share of beggars and sad cases. We deal. Has to be the way.'

'You think they've got anything worth trading? They're walking corpses. Hal barely has a roof on his house.'

'I'll talk to the leader. Even a gesture would help. Can't have us seen to be giving handouts.'

Gryffin nods. Klay's right. Doesn't mean he feels good about taking from people who've already lost so much. 'Fine. Get the supplies ready. We'll stay overnight. I left a team fixing the pipe to the main well. They've had no easy access to water since the attack. See what else we can do before we leave. Take a look at Hal's roof. Next heavy rain he'll drown in his bed.'

'Yes, sir. I'll get this lot sorted then head over to the town.'

Gryffin watches as Klay tells Chayse and the other two men the news. Chayse looks up at him, a wide smile on his face. Gryffin groans to himself. The first job - wipe that smile off his face. Shouldn't be too difficult.

36

Bray shouts and sits up quickly. He yelps in pain as his head bangs against the bulkhead above him.

'Hey, take it easy.'

The voice sounds familiar but the woolly feeling in his brain is stopping anything of sense from getting through. 'What...' His weak croak is barely audible. He clears his throat and tries again. 'Where...'

He is lowered back onto the bed and something cool is placed on his forehead. 'You were given something to help you sleep while we got you out. As for the where - you're on my shuttle.'

It all comes back to Bray in a rush. He remembers

the meeting with Hank, being taken out of his cell by the guard. 'You drugged me?' He opens his eyes to glare at Hank. The man is sitting on a bench seat on the opposite side of the small hold.

'Heath had no choice. We were running out of time and from what he said, you were not keen on getting into the box.'

Bray closes his eyes to stop the room from spinning. 'How long will I feel like shit?'

Hank laughs. 'About thirty minutes. Just stay where you are and rest. You've been through a lot.'

Bray raises his hand to rub his eyes. Thirty minutes of wooziness definitely beats life in prison. 'How many guards are on your payroll?'

Hank nods to the cockpit. Bray lifts his head and sees Heath at the helm. 'Just one. Heath kindly agreed to help get you out. We managed to get him onto the staff a few months ago. It takes time to work up to a position on the housing levels. Maintenance was the only option. I think it worked out well.'

Bray drops his head back on the pillow. 'Yeah, for you.'

'For you too, Brayden.'

'Just Bray. Only one person calls me Brayden, and it's not you.'

Hank nods. 'Very well. Bray it is.'

'So, care to share why things are going to work out well for me? I mean, I appreciate you getting me out. I owe you for that. Think I deserve to know why you went to all that trouble.'

Hank looks down at his clasped hands. 'I made a serious mistake quite a few years ago and I need your help to fix it.'

Bray snorts. 'Right, that explains everything. Thanks.'

Hanks ignores his comment as he focuses on a spot on the floor. His eyes stay fixed to it as he speaks. 'Did you know that in some cultures, the word chaos refers to the void state preceding the creation of the universe.' Bray shrugs not knowing where he's going.

'The Foundation is attempting to create an idealistic universe from the chaos they perceive around them. Their statement - not mine. Chaos.' He laughs harshly and shakes his head. 'The Sectors are only in chaos because of the Foundation. Their ideal universe is a lie. The assigning of positions, the arranged marriages, where you can live. It's all so they can ensure they have people they deem worthy or useful within reach. That is why the Outer Sector was populated in the first place. It was the first major relocation of those the Foundation didn't approve of.'

'Yeah, I know all that. You don't need to be a Foundation hotshot to know what they're doing. What's all this got to do with me? As much as I'd like to, I don't reckon I can take down the Council. Fuck it. I'm willing to give it a shot if you can get me close enough.'

Hank nods. 'I have no doubt you would. What you don't know about the Foundation's plans is what they have been creating for years behind the back of the populace. Cyborgs.'

Bray waits for the punchline that never comes. The Foundation may be void of any sense of right and wrong, but creating cyborgs is a whole other league. 'Okay. Why would they do that?'

'Defence mainly. The Foundation have security personnel, but their numbers are pitiful. If they truly plan to continue their mass relocations, they would face resistance.'

'So why not just leave everyone where they are?'

'Earth is reaching her limit. The Council must do something drastic if she is to survive for future generations. Their future generations. They have no intention of changing how they live, changing where they live. The only solution they see is to move some of the population to the Outer Sector. Unless they increase their security quite substantially, they will struggle to physically stand up to the many objections they will receive.'

'So why not just hire more security?'

'From the local population?' Avoca shakes his head. 'They risk having their security turn against them when faced with displacing their own family or friends. No, the only solution they... we, could see was to make sure the security personnel would be completely obedient to the Council. So the project began.'

Bray nods but doesn't say anything. What the hell can he say to that? Either the man is telling the truth - which is scary and not something he wants to think about, or Bray's stuck on a transport with someone a tad unstable.

'I see you need a little more convincing.' He pauses and wrings his hands together. 'What I am about to tell you could end so much more than just my career. My life would be over if anyone knew I was speaking to you.'

'Didn't get a lot of time for socialising on Tyrat. You can safely assume I don't know anyone.'

Avoca nods and takes a deep breath. 'I have little choice either way. This project – it is not a new venture. For several years they – apologies – we, have been experimenting with cybernetics. The aim was to create technology that, when fitted, would give us control over the subject. For reasons I cannot fathom, I helped set up the project with a few of my colleagues. I'm not going to say I didn't know what I was getting in to. Deep down I must have realised what this would mean for those we picked for the project. When the time came to test the devices it was too late to back out. I stood by as the first batch of test subjects was brought in. Unwilling test subjects.'

Bray's eyes narrow as the man continues.

'Of course they were unwilling. Who would volunteer for something like that. I should have known from the beginning that would be the case, but I didn't allow myself to think about it.'

'Where were they taken from?'

'Ships. We paid.. we paid Slavers to attack various ships and bring the...'

'The innocent people.' Bray finishes the sentence for him.

Avoca licks his lips. 'Yes. They were brought to the location and were worked on. Our scientist...' Avoca closes his eyes and shakes his head. He doesn't attempt to elaborate which suits Bray just fine.

'The project came to an end when the station used for the procedures was destroyed, presumably with the loss of all lives on board. The Foundation considered it a premature end. I, however, could not have been more pleased. It should never have been started in the first place. The files were sealed and the project was left to haunt my dreams.

'That was where it remained until very recently. I found out one of these subjects survived. It's only a matter of time before the Foundation finds out he's alive and comes after him to finish what they started. I need your help to design something to counteract the control implant that was fitted in his head so he cannot be used as intended.'

Bray rises to his elbows, waiting until Hank looks at him before he speaks. 'Wait. You need me to what?'

'I know you can do it. I've checked your records.'

'I don't have records.'

Hank takes a unit off the bench and passes it to Bray. Bray scans through the data and his mouth drops open. Every detail of his life is on the screen in his hands. Hank having details of his time on Earth, Bray understands. The Foundation doesn't erase anything. It's his exploits on Vana, and after, that surprises him. 'How did you get all this? I was off the radar.'

Hank smiles sheepishly. 'There's no such thing, Bray. The Foundation has eyes and ears everywhere. I just knew which contacts to approach.'

Bray swings his legs around and places his feet on the ground. 'What does my asshole of a brother have to do with all this? Was he...' Bray pauses and swallows as the question jams in his throat. 'Was he one of the test people?'

Avoca frowns as he rubs the back of his neck. 'Interesting term to use. Were... are you not close?'

Bray snorts. 'Close? We were until he pulled a disappearing act and tore my fucking family apart.'

Avoca looks at the ground and nods once. 'I see. I did not realise you felt that way.'

'Why the hell would you know? You may have my records but that doesn't mean you know me. Anyway, you didn't answer my question. Was he one of them?'

Avoca focuses on his clasped hands for a long time before he finally nods. 'I am deeply sorry to tell you this but Daegan was part of the... part of the second shipment. I received notification from the man running the project. Several children were injured during the initial attack on the transport. Your brother was one of the casualties. He died on his way to the station. The small consolation is that those few children never saw that place.'

Bray swallows and looks out the front of the transport. So, he's finally got the confirmation he's wanted for years. Daegan is dead. It's done. So why doesn't he feel any better? Why isn't the pain going away? Then it hits him. His parents died looking for someone who was already dead. What a fucking waste.

'So, let me get this straight. You kidnapped my brother along with his whole class so you could turn them into cyborgs? And now you expect me to help you finish that. You're out of your fucking mind. You killed my brother. What makes you think I'm not going to return the favour.'

Avoca holds up his hands. 'I cannot blame you. No amount of wishing will let me change the past. All I can do is try to stop this from happening all over again. I need your help for that.'

Bray glares across at the man who managed to save his life then followed it by tearing a hole in his chest. A hole he took a long time trying to close. He doesn't want to think about what Daegan would have gone through as part of some secret experiment. Avoca is right about that part. Knowing he died on the school transport is a consolation of sorts. The alternative... it's more than he can deal with right now. 'Are you... damn it. Are you sure he's dead? Maybe he got out or...'

'Each of the children was given an identifying mark on their way to the station. I was sent the list of names along with their identifying numbers. I'm sorry, Bray, but Daegan is dead.'

Avoca remains silent for a few moments as Bray tries to get his head around everything he's just been told. He always knew the Foundation and corruption went together, but this takes things to a whole new level. They were delving into areas most of the hardened criminals he dealt with couldn't stomach. And they're going to do it again.

'So, you've got this elaborate plan to right all your wrongs and stop the Foundation from doing this again. Why me? There must be hundreds, thousands of people more qualified than me. I'm a glorified mechanic and weapons dealer.'

'According to the information I found, you're a lot more than that. You are the person I need.'

Bray gets to his feet, placing a hand on the ceiling above him to steady himself. 'Either the drug is still messing with my head or you're not making any sense. How can I possibly be who you need?'

Hank stands up and faces him. 'I need someone with no ties to the Foundation. Someone with the... let's just say someone with a colourful background. Someone who won't stand out.'

'Stand out where? I'm not going back to Earth. I'll take the prison over that.'

Hank frowns but shakes his head. 'You would rather prison?'

'Long story. But you probably know all that, right? You know everything else.'

Hank ignores him. 'I need someone who can blend in with a new group recently formed in the Outer Sector - the Hunters.'

Bray quietly looks at him before he breaks out

laughing. 'Hunters? Why not just kill me right now.'

'You are a perfect fit for them.'

'It's not that. It's the Nomad I'm worried about.'

Hank shakes his head, frowning. 'I don't understand.'

'I thought you knew everything? I was in prison and I heard about it. Sayber, the leader of the Hunters, used to be a Nomad. He tried to decapitate his captain. Barely got out alive. Now he's calling himself a Hunter. Wants to hunt Nomad or something like that. I don't know. What I do know is that when he mutinied, he pissed off a lot of Nomad, including the leader. From what I heard on Tyrat, he's not someone you mess with.'

'You know about him?'

'The Nomad leader? Only snippets. He's the first person to escape Tyrat prison - well, until now.'

Hank nods. 'He's the survivor of the project.'

'Damn,' Bray mutters. 'You know what? It makes sense. Could explain a lot.' Bray risks a few steps and is relieved when he doesn't fall flat on his face. The drug must be working out of his system. 'Okay, let me get this straight. You want me to join the Hunters, sworn enemies of the Nomad, so I can work on a block to the control implant in the Nomad leader's head.'

'More or less.'

'So why not join the Nomad?'

'I'm assuming that, once my colleagues find out, the Nomad leader will be targeted and taken to the Hunters. There's no way they could risk keeping him on a Nomad ship. There are too many people loyal to him. Besides, the Hunters are still finding their feet in the Sector. They are still open to recruits. The Nomad have always been difficult if not near impossible to join. Even if they do recruit, the odds of being assigned to the same ship as the leader are slim. It could take years to work up to a posting on his ship. We don't have that time.'

'So why not just tell this guy what's going to happen and… I don't know, maybe ask him if you can fit the block.'

'I can't do anything. The people I'm working for have eyes and ears everywhere. You have no idea of the lengths I had to go to just to get you out.' He nods to the screen Bray left of the bench. 'That has the schematics of the implant fitted to him. It's not as easy as loading the block and he'll be fixed. The programming is complex. I'm not an expert, but I've been told it's not something that can be rectified in one sitting. It also has to be done in such a way as to not attract attention to us… or to him for that matter. If the Foundation finds out what we're doing, they could rectify it before we're finished.'

'I like the way you said 'we'. I haven't agreed to anything yet. You're asking a hell of a lot of me. Leaving all this Nomad cyborg stuff aside, getting onto the Hunter ship will be hard enough.'

'Not for you. Bray, you're young, have just escaped Tyrat where you honed your fighting skills, much to my horror, and have no family or friends in the area.

Where else would you go?'

Bray glares at him for a moment. It doesn't paint a great picture when put like that. He slumps back onto the bench and looks through the schematics, not taking the information in. Hank is right, it's not like he has anything else to do. Being part of the Hunter crew could be the lifeline he needs. 'How long will I need to stay there?'

Hank shakes his head. 'Hard to say.'

'And you don't want to tell him? It might speed things up if this cyborg was working with us.'

Hank shakes his head again. 'It's best this way. I'm hoping I'll be able to do something from the inside before any of this becomes a problem. I only want to use this as a last resort.' He pauses and takes a deep breath. 'This project has already put him through too much.'

Bray makes a face as he looks out the window. He needs to do this. Apart from a second shot at a life away from Tyrat and the many mistakes he's made, he needs to do it for his parents. They died looking for Daegan. As much as he hates his brother for insisting on going on the fucking trip in the first place, he owes it to his mum and dad to stop the Foundation destroying any more families. 'Damn it. Fine. I'll do it.'

Hank lets out a huge breath. 'Thank you, Bray. That's great news.'

'One condition.'

Hank's smile fades slightly. 'Go on.'

'You got somewhere I can get cleaned up and grab

some clothes? I've been in these for months. I'm seriously offending myself, so fuck knows how you two are managing.'

'Didn't want to put a downer on your great escape,' Heath says from the cockpit, 'but you do stink, mate.'

37

Gryffin seals the last crate of medical supplies and loads it onto the transport. His crew had worked tirelessly, helping to repair as many houses as possible. They had also restored the supply to the main well, bringing water back to each of the houses. It wasn't much, but the way the locals were reacting it was like he was leaving crates of credits on their doorsteps.

'That's the last one. Unload it and straight back. I want to get out of here.'

The transport takes off, moving towards the town a few miles away. Gryffin frowns as a deep rumble replaces the hum of the transports engines. He looks out the back of the ship. There's a dust cloud heading in their direction. A few minutes later, a large motorbike comes to a stop at the base of the ramp. The rider removes his visor and dismounts. Hal dusts off his clothes and runs a rag over the paintwork. 'Klay said it was all right to come here. I hope you don't mind.'

Gryffin walks down the ramp and frowns behind his mask at Hal. 'Problem?'

'Far from it.' Hal gestures to the bike and smiles. 'Klay asked if there was anything we could give as payment for the help. A gesture of sorts. This was my son's.' His smile drops. 'He passed away two years ago. He won it in a card game. I have no idea where the losing player got it from.' He shrugs. 'It has been gathering dust in my shed since he passed. I have no use for it.'

Gryffin walks around the machine. It's stunning. The black paint is pristine. He stops when he gets to the side. There's a purple griffin painted on the side. An identical match to the one towering over the loading ramp of *Ares*. 'When I suggested this as payment Klay assured me it would be well received. I took the liberty of ensuring you would be less inclined to turn it down.'

'I'm not taking it. Your son left it to you.'

'And as I said, I have no use for it.'

'Sell it then. Use the credits on yourself.'

'I have tried. No one wants or can afford a machine

like this. We need food and medical supplies. Something like this is useless on our world. Please, Captain. You and your men have brought us from the brink of...' he pauses and looks at the bike again. 'We will survive now. Take this as a thank you. Please.' He hands Gryffin a piece of paper. 'The code for the engine. Enjoy it, Captain. I must go back and ensure the supplies you have given us are properly stored away.'

The old man turns away and walks back towards the town, leaving Gryffin staring after him. He looks down at the bike again and runs his gloved hand over the griffin emblem.

The motorbike is stunning. Weapons, food, and medical supplies are always welcome, but getting the bike is in a whole other league. He's never had anything that's just his. He may have command of *Ares*, but she's home to the rest of the crew. The bike is his and his alone. A first for him. He runs his hand along her deep brown leather saddle and manages to suppress the smile. Gryffin swings his leg over the saddle and keys the sequence of numbers into the control panel. The bike roars to life and this time the smile comes out.

38

'What is this place?'

Avoca ignores Bray as he manoeuvres the shuttle through the gaping cargo doors leading into the space station. Exhausted by his efforts to get Bray out, Heath had taken to one of the bunks a few hours into their journey leaving Avoca at the helm. Bray fights the urge to take the controls from the older man. Watching him pilot the shuttle is like watching Morgan do it. How they got here in one piece is a damn miracle.

Once safely inside, Bray relaxes slightly. Or does until he looks out the front of the craft. The station is a far cry from the abandoned shell they were heading towards. State of the art docking bays line the levels of the gigantic hold, offering berth for at least four cruiser-sized vessels. 'You going to tell me where we are?'

Avoca smiles and gestures for Bray to follow. It takes two attempts to convince his weak body to rise from the comfortable seat. He shuffles after Avoca, blinking as the bright lights assault his eyes. A strangely dressed couple hurry towards them.

'Bray, I'd like to introduce the people who made your escape possible. This is Evie and Felix Dixon.'

The couple facing him couldn't be more eccentric if they tried. They must be in their mid to late sixties and are two of the most unimposing people he's ever seen. Evie's wiry grey hair is escaping from beneath a wide-brimmed straw hat with the most ridiculous flower sticking from the top. Her over-sized red jumper has more holes than a garment should have and her knee length green skirt is patched in three places. The brown sandals make an irritating slapping sound as she hurries towards them, one hand on her hat to stop it falling off.

Following closely behind, Felix Dixon's green cargo shorts, blazer, rumpled shirt and socks with sandals combo is just as impressive.

'How long have they been out here?' Bray whispers as the couple hurry towards them, mumbling to each other.

'They're a decent couple, just not too caught up on

Foundation fashions.'

Felix holds out his hand, shaking Avoca's vigorously. 'So, this is the stray you want to re-home? Not much to look at is he?'

Evie slaps her husband on the chest. 'Not in front of him. Where are your manners?' She smiles and holds out her hand. Bray stares at her outstretched hand. 'You want me to kiss it?'

'Well, I don't want you to shake it.'

Bray takes her hand and kisses it quickly. She pats him on the shoulder. 'What excellent manners. Now, forgive my bluntness, dear but you look like you've been to hell and back. How does a hot shower, clean bed and a good meal, consisting of real food I might add, sound to you?'

Bray eyes the couple suspiciously for a moment but finally shrugs. After what just happened and after spending the best part of two years in Tyrat, it sounds pretty damn fantastic. 'Good, thanks.'

Evie claps her hands together. 'Splendid.' She waves at Heath. 'Welcome back... you.'

'My name is Heath.'

'Yes, of course it is. So, did you enjoy your holiday on Tyrat?'

Heath takes his fake Tyrat ID and passes to Felix. 'It wasn't exactly a holiday. The place is... well, not good. Fair play surviving there for two years. You've got my respect.'

Bray turns to look at him. 'You know them?'

Heath nods. 'I've worked for them for a bit.

Avoca needed someone to go in and get you out. Sorry about tranqing you. Time wasn't on our side and you didn't look too keen on getting into the box.'

Bray closes his eyes and a chill runs through his body. He'd still be on Tyrat if Heath hadn't knocked him out. 'No problem. Thanks for getting me out.'

Heath slaps him on the back, apologising when he nearly knocks Bray off his feet. 'I'll get you some grub. Second thoughts, I'll have a shower first. I can still smell that place. The smell of rot has gotten into my pores.'

Evie links arms with Bray and guides him towards the double doors at the far side of the hangar. 'Well, Bray. Why don't you come with me for a bit? I just want to give you a quick check. Make sure you're not going to keel over on us after going to all that trouble.'

'What is this place?'

Avoca falls into step beside Evie and Bray while Felix takes the ID from Evie and disappears through another door. 'The Dixon's are dear, dear friends of mine,' Hank explains. 'Their little enterprise operates outside Foundation rules.'

'What enterprise?'

'We help people in need,' Evie replies.

'By breaking them out of Foundation prison?'

Hank pauses as Evie keys in a code to get through the door. 'Not just that. They dabble in a variety of specialities. If I'm being honest, I don't fully understand what they do.'

'For a reason,' Evie interrupts. 'Can't have every

Tom, Dick, and Harry knowing our business. Nothing covert about being in the public eye.' She winks at Bray and hums to herself as she guides him through the base.

Avoca smiles at her but she's in her own world again. 'What I do know is that you are safe here, Bray. The Foundation will not find you here. No one will.'

Evie stops at a large door labelled Med Bay. 'Hank, you go get yourself dinner. I'll see to Bray and meet you in a bit. That sound okay to you, Bray?'

Bray nods, too sore and tired to care about anything at the moment. For now, he'll do what he's told. Food and sleep are all he wants to think about. He's no idiot. They didn't go to that much effort and expense to break him out so he can eat and sleep for months - as much as he'd like to. If he's going to have a chance in hell of convincing the Hunter captain to take him on, he'll need a miracle.

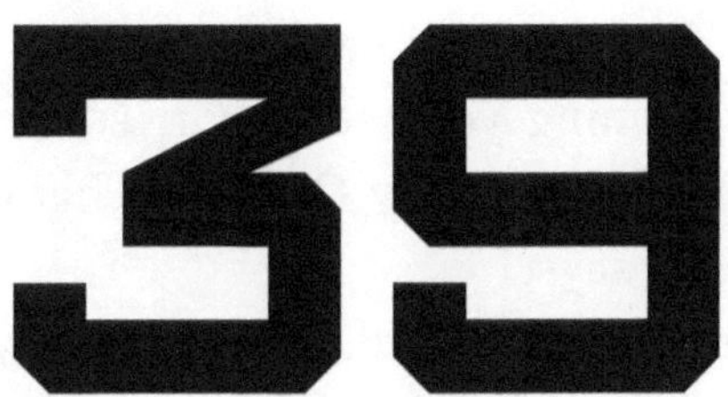

DIXON SPACE STATION

'Excuse me?' Felix leans on the table as he glares over at Avoca.

'I didn't tell him his brother's still alive.'

Evie mutters into her husband's ear. The man nods then looks at Avoca again. 'My wife and I are in complete agreement. I'll backfire on you – you know that.'

'Of course I do but I was left with little choice. As soon as I mentioned his brother, Bray's demeanour changed. He holds quite a lot of resentment towards Daegan.'

'For being kidnapped?' Evie says.

'For disappearing and sending his life into a spiral of pain, loss, and Tyrat.'

Felix snorts loudly. 'Yeah. Like he wasn't responsible for his own actions. Can't blame a dead guy for everything that went wrong.'

'I know that,' Avoca says. 'It's how he feels so there's little I can do to change that.'

'I'm presuming you were worried Bray wouldn't agree to help if he knew Gryffin is his long-lost big brother,' Evie says.

'Precisely. I know I will answer for my decision at some stage, but for now, it was the right move. Brayden can't know Gryffin's true identity. It won't help either of them.'

'Very well,' Felix replies. 'So, young Bray is, for want of a better description, a walking corpse. You know getting him fit and healthy will take time. He's starving, dehydrated, covered in old and new wounds and I won't hazard a guess as to what's living in that hair of his. He can barely lift a knife and fork let alone a weapon.'

'Can you help him?'

'Of course we can,' Evie says. 'Heath isn't head of our security because he makes a mean cocktail. Seriously, I recommend you try one. They're exquisite. Anyway, he's a dab hand at combat. Trained by the best in the Foundation security services. Their loss our gain. He'll whip your boy into shape. I can handle the medical side. It'll take time to get his body strong enough to go up against Heath.'

'I understand. Time isn't on our side, however.'

'Timing in this matter will be down to Bray and how fast he recovers.' Evie pushes a lock of hair back under her hat. 'I'll pop him in a rejuvenation pod for a spell. That should give him a boost. We'll see where we go from there.' She gets to her feet and saunters towards the door. 'First things first. The lad needs a bowl of my famous soup.'

DIXON SPACE STATION

Bray wipes a hand over the mirror and grips the side of the sink to support himself. The reflection of a stranger looks back at him. No wonder Avoca wasn't sure he was the one he was looking for. Bray is having a hard time accepting he's looking at himself. His brown hair reaches his shoulders and is thick with heavy clumps of matted knots. His beard is just as bad, and even though the first shower he took was laced with a suitable insecticide, he swears something is still crawling in it. He'd never been broad or big, but prided himself on being fit and worked out regularly to keep himself that way. Or did until his time in the crate. All that work has withered away to leave a skeletal frame that can barely support itself let alone any muscle mass.

He opens the drawer under the sink and takes out the scissors and clippers. Time to give any remaining hitchhikers nowhere to hide.

A good fifteen minutes later he brushes his hand over his tightly shaved head, relieved to be rid of all that hair. The beard is gone, exposing sunken cheeks and a sickly complexion. Before anything can escape from the removed hair, he shoves it into the disposal unit and showers again, just to be sure.

He finds a fresh set of clothes and dresses, taking a ridiculously long time to do the simple task. Completely exhausted, he sits on the edge of the bed and stares at his hands. A gentle knock on the door brings him out of his daze. 'Yeah?'

Evie Dixon steps inside, a heavily laden tray in her hands. 'Thought you might appreciate food coming to you instead of having to go get it. Have to say, I was half expecting you to collapse in the shower.'

'Nearly did.'

She places the tray on the dresser beside his bed and turns to examine him. 'You look better but also so much worse. Strange.'

He can't help but laugh. 'I feel better and worse. Thank you for doing this.'

She brushes his comment away. 'Don't be ridiculous. Any enemy of the Foundation is a friend of ours. So, I trust your confinement was difficult?'

Bray smiles weakly. 'It wasn't fun.'

Evie nods and places a hand on his arm, squeezing gently. 'Well, that's behind you now. The most important thing is to get you up and about again. That starts with a good meal. I've kept it to soup and bread for now. All freshly made, mind you. None of this reconstituted rubbish the Foundation serves. Once your stomach can handle that, we'll try something more adventurous. Eat, then get yourself into bed and stay there.'

She gets up and looks critically at him. 'You need anything else?'

'I'm good. Nothing some food and sleep can't fix.'

'Glad to hear it. I'll leave you to it. You're safe here, Brayden. The Foundation doesn't know we're here. You can trust us. We're batty, but all the good people are.' With a chuckle, she turns and leaves him to his food.

He doesn't know how he does it, but he remains civil while he's eating. He's not a caged animal anymore. Time he starts acting human again.

DIXON SPACE STATION

Bray curses as he lands heavily on his knees.

'Get up.'

He looks up at Heath and shakes his head. 'I need five.'

Heath holds out his hand, pulling Bray to his feet. 'No, you don't. You're doing damn well, Bray. But you need to keep pushing yourself.'

'What the fuck do you think I'm doing?'

'Brayden!'

He winces as Evie's shrill scream stops both men in their tracks. He's in for a world of trouble and Heath knows it too if his expression is anything to go by.

'You curse like that again and I will personally package you up and send you back to Tyrat.' She winks at him softening her words.

'I'm sorry, Evie.'

'As well you should be. What exactly is the problem?'

'I'm tired.'

'Heath. Go away.'

She waits until he has done just that before she looks at Bray again. 'You need to push yourself, Bray. You're letting your body dictate, when it's none of its business.'

'Do you even listen to yourself?'

'Rarely.' She taps the side of his head. 'You're strong, Bray. There's no way you would have survived the crate that long if you weren't. We're trying to get your body to that same level.'

'It's not working. I've been training for weeks and I still look like a damn skeleton. There's no chance in hell the Hunters will see me as an asset.'

'Of course they won't.'

'Thanks for that.'

'What do you expect? You're giving up. Hank gave us a copy of your prison records. I'm having a hard time matching that record with you. According to the lovely officers tasked with your care, you were a favourite in the fighting rings. Earned quite a badge of honour. Where's that Bray?'

'That Bray was fighting for his life.'

'So is this one. The Foundation is slowly killing

people. Whether through this project or by other means, that is their goal. Only a certain group of people are deemed worthy. Everyone else is on borrowed time. Do you think you would be one of those lucky few? What about your family? Morgan, Erin and Shayla aren't one of the elite. They're expendable. Just like you are. Your body is capable. Your mind is capable. You just need them to work together. If it helps, put yourself back in Tyrat. Use that anger. Use the frustration. Use that as motivation. Use that to make you stronger.'

'That easy, huh?'

Evie snorts loudly. 'If it was that easy, I'd be a damn warrior princess. No. It's far from easy. It's going to be bloody hard work, but what I'm saying is that you have a solid foundation. That gives you the advantage.'

Bray sighs and wipes a hand over his face. She's right. He knows it and so does the irritating woman. The problem is he has no confidence in himself. Surviving Tyrat was just that - surviving. He didn't do anything special, it was just damn luck. If Avoca hadn't freed him, he'd still be in that box... or dead. It didn't take any skills to get where he is now. He was just in the right place at the right time.

'You lose it in Tyrat or before?'

'Lose what?'

'Your guts. Your nerve. Whatever you want to call it.'

'I haven't lost it.'

'Is that so. Prove it.'

42

'We've managed to do a little creative mastery on your record.'

Bray sits at the far end of the wide table in the meeting room and stares at the screen in front of him. 'I still have a Foundation record?'

Evie makes a face. 'Yes and no. I'm not quite sure how to tell you this, Bray, but you're dead.'

'I'm what?'

'Dead. A goner. Space waste-'

'Yes, thank you, Felix.' Evie glares at him them smiles as she focuses on Bray again. 'As my delightful husband so nicely put it, you're dead. When Avoca and

Heath removed you from Tyrat, the Foundation decided to cover up the hilariously embarrassing situation with a bit of fiction. According to your official record, you perished in an illegal fight with another prisoner. Naughty boy. So, you're dead.'

Bray nods slowly. He knew he was as good as dead when he went to Tyrat, but having it as an official entry on his record is another thing. 'Have my family been told?'

The Dixon's look at each other briefly. 'I'm afraid so, dear,' Evie says. 'They were told a week or so after they decided on the lie to tell. We've only just found out. I am sorry.'

Bray smiles but it's far from genuine. 'Probably best. Clean break for them.' At least now they won't be wondering where he is or what he's doing. They've also had to deal with two dead nephews with no graves.

'Do you need a few minutes?' Felix asks.

'Thanks, but I'm good. So, what creative mastery have you done?'

'Okay, for starters we altered your arrest date just in case the Hunters can access the data. If anyone asks you were in there for five years. Makes you look like more of a tough guy. Not many survive in there that long and then escape.'

'Right. But if they can access my records they'll also find out I'm dead. Won't that be a problem?'

'It would if we didn't make it look like there was a cover-up. With a little digging, it wouldn't be difficult to find you escaped. The Foundation won't be looking to cover up something they've already covered up. All we did is restore some internal communications between the guards and the Foundation about your untimely exit. Believe me, it won't do your credibility any harm. What also works in our favour is how you spent your time in Tyrat.'

Felix pauses as he brings up Bray's prison record. 'Don't like playing with others, do you? You were in a fight every day.'

'Had to find some way of passing the time.'

'Earned yourself a total of eight months in the isolation cell though. Was it worth it?'

Bray stares at the data on the screen. Eight months in total? He knew he'd spent his fair share of time in there but never thought it was that long. The hairs on his arms stand to attention when he remembers the suffocating confines of the metal box.

'Are you still with us?'

'What?'

Evie leans closer to him. 'You went back there for a second.'

'Didn't know it was that long. Probably should have behaved myself.'

Felix waves a hand dismissively. 'Where's the fun in that? Anyway, this record mixed with everything you did before you were arrested will make you very attractive to the Hunters. I must admit, it makes you very attractive to us. You'd make a fine addition to our team, but Hank made us promise we wouldn't steal you.'

'I owe him - for now.'

Felix winks at him. 'Indeed - for now. We've both had a chat with Heath and he's impressed with your progress. You had impressive combat skills, just a little rough around the edges.'

Evie nods in agreement. 'I must say the emaciated skeleton look didn't suit you. I much prefer this buff version.'

Felix rolls his eyes as his wife smiles at Bray. 'Oh, would you knock it off, woman.'

Bray ignores the couple as they go through one of their many squabbles. Despite the fact it was pointed out by someone old enough to be his mother, he takes the compliment.

It's been two months since Avoca helped him escape Tyrat. The time was spent recovering from months of abuse and malnutrition. Every morning, under the instruction of Heath, Bray had been worked hard. Although Heath was only a few years older, the man had years of experience on Bray. Muscles he never knew existed screamed after every training session and he was lucky if he made it to his bunk before he collapsed of exhaustion after the sessions. If Bray asked to stop, Heath would just push him harder.

The shell of a man Heath took from the prison is a distant memory. Working out and eating three large meals a day had done wonders for his body. He'd put on weight - most of it muscle and is fitter than he's ever been. You'd be hard-pressed to find many similarities between the two versions of himself.

After his gruelling morning, Bray would refuel on a large lunch made by Evie before Felix took over his training. The rest of the day was spent looking over schematics of the implants the Foundation's scientist had designed. Thanks to the Dixon's connections, he also had access to a lot of data on the Hunters and Nomad. Bray knows everything he needs to know about Sayber and the Hunters. More importantly, he also knows about Gryffin and what he needs to alter in his programming to block the Foundation from implanting their own program. Well, in theory. The practice part would have to wait until he was face-to-face with the Nomad captain. Whatever happens with Gryffin and the program is out of his hands. For now, he's been given a second chance at life and there's nothing he will do to mess it up.

He crosses his arms and watches the couple play through one of their many squabbles, but grows impatient. 'Hey. Hey!'

The couple stops and turns to face him. 'What?'

'Sayber? Have you found him yet?'

Evie frowns then nods. 'Ah, yes. Sayber. Why do all these Hunter and Nomad have such inventive names? We think we may have found him. Since his unsuccessful takeover of *Ares*, he's been keeping to himself. He's got himself a ship. I believe it's called *Perses*. He's got some crew but is looking to recruit.'

'Is he a serious threat to the Nomad?'

'A threat - yes. Serious one - not so much. Gryffin has got himself a few dozen ships. That number can't be confirmed of course. The Nomad are shrouded in secrets. It's hard to get a grasp on the figures. The contention between Sayber and Gryffin will fuel most of the motivation to cause the Nomad issues. It's no secret Sayber wants to finish what he started when he cut Gryffin's throat.'

'Is there a chance they'll kill each other before the Foundation finds out about Gryffin being one of their creations?'

Evie makes a face. 'Anything is possible.'

'So, when do I get to sell myself to Sayber?'

Felix leans back in his chair and rests his feet on the table. 'Avoca is planning for two weeks, tops. He's going to join us in a week or so and have a look over the final details. He'll want to see a working program you can upload to Gryffin. You've got till then to finalise any plans you have for the program and get more training in place. Sound good?'

'Sounds good. Just hope I can convince Sayber I'm a fit.'

'Have a little faith,' Evie says. 'You're ready. He needs people like you for his crew. It'll be like all his birthdays have come at once when you saunter into his world.'

43

'That's him?'

Avoca takes a sip of his drink and places the tumbler back on the sticky bar top. 'That's Sayber. Leader of the newly formed Hunters.'

Bray discretely examines the Hunter leader over the rim of his chipped glass. The tall man could easily blend into the crowd filling the bar. Unless you were looking closely, there's nothing special about him. Nothing to give you a hint to his true identity. But Bray knows differently. To the untrained eye, he's just another down and out worker, but Bray sees him for what he is - a deadly leader.

Sayber raises his glass to take a sip of his drink, and Bray instantly notices the large scar spreading from the man's right thumb to disappear under the sleeve of his shirt. After months of study, Bray knows Gryffin gave Sayber that scar after he broke away from the Nomad. Sayber's dark eyes never stop moving, even when deep in conversation with the man opposite him. His back is to the corner, the two main doors in the bar within sight at all times. His hand rests casually on his hip in easy reach of the gun and knife strapped to his belt. Can't blame him. Being at the top of the Nomad's wanted list isn't somewhere he'd want to be.

Bray takes another mouthful of ale as he looks around the bar. 'You sure you don't want to go over and chat with him yourself?'

Avoca rolls his eyes at Bray's smirk. 'Thanks for the offer, but I think I'll leave this bit to you.' His expression turns sombre as he faces Bray. 'Last chance. Are you sure you're ready for this?'

'It's what you got me out for.'

'True, but if you're not sure, if anyone suspects or doubts you... I don't want...'

'Hey, this will be easy compared to Tyrat. I can handle it. I'm not going to get myself killed. Well, not intentionally.' Bray laughs at the look of horror on Avoca's face. 'Relax, you'll give yourself a heart attack.'

'You're the one who's going to give it to me.' Avoca looks over at the group of Hunters again and presses his lips together. Eventually, he nods slowly and looks back to Bray. 'I guess this is it then. Don't forget to send me any information that seems pertinent.'

Bray finishes his drink. 'I got it. Seriously, Avoca. I got it.'

'Good luck.'

Bray smirks and walks away, allowing the crowd to swallow him. He makes his way over to the Hunters at the same time as one of the locals. The short, squat man wipes beer off his chin as he stumbles towards Sayber. Bray keeps Sayber and the man in his sight as he pushes through the drunken crowd. Timing is vital. If he's off by even a few seconds, he'll lose his chance. The man nears Sayber, forcefully shoving through the bodies around him. The man draws his weapon and raises his arm. Bray clears the last few steps quickly.

'Hunter!' The man's scream cuts through the noise in the bar. Bray launches himself at Sayber as the man fires his weapon. His body hits Sayber's with such force, the air is driven from his lungs. They crash to the ground as the bullet punches into the wall where Sayber's head was less than a second ago. Bray doesn't get a chance to recover before he is hauled off the Hunter captain by the rest of his men. Three men pin him to the ground as another two help Sayber to his feet. The Hunter leader points his weapon at the man who tried to attack him, but a security team gets to them before he can fire.

'Where the hell are you taking him?'

They ignore him and drag the man away. Sayber's steely gaze follows the man from the room. Avoca called the guards at the right time. If it had taken them a few seconds longer to reach the bar, the attacker's help would have been rewarded by a bullet to the head.

Sayber turns his attention from the retreating guards to Bray. He nods once at the men restraining Bray, and they slowly release him. Bray dusts off his clothes then stands tall in front of Sayber. The Hunter examines him, his eyes moving from Bray's scuffed boots and up his worn trousers to his cracked leather jacket. Sayber's eyes come to a stop on his face and Bray feels a little uncomfortable under the scrutiny. Bray and Avoca had made sure every detail of Bray's outfit and appearance would fit with his cover. The details weren't too difficult to remember. Apart from the fact Avoca broke him out of prison, everything else is true. He got wrapped up with the wrong people, ended up in Tyrat and then escaped.

Bray should turn away from Sayber. Avoca told him to respect Sayber, make the man think he'll be an obedient fit for his crew, but Bray's stubborn streak isn't playing ball. Tyrat had conditioned him to stand up for himself. Fight or die. He holds his head high and takes a step closer to Sayber. 'Great security you have. They nearly got you a bullet to the head.'

Sayber's eyes widen and he tilts his head to the side. One of the Hunters with him growls and takes a step closer. Sayber holds up his hand, stopping the man in his tracks. 'Is that so? What makes you think they wouldn't have stopped it?'

Bray laughs. 'You got to see it coming if you're going to stop it.' He looks over at the team behind Sayber and makes a face. 'These guys were too busy drinking your profits away to notice anything going on around them.'

Sayber crosses his arms and smirks. 'What do you want?'

'Nothing. The question is - what do you need?'

'Let me guess, you're here to tell me, right?'

'You have a ship?'

Sayber nods slowly.

'In that case, you need me. I can do a better job than these idiots put together.'

'You want a job?' Sayber asks over the murmurs of anger from his men.

Bray shrugs. 'Let's just say I need to get away from the border and further into the Outer Sector. I'll watch your back in exchange for free passage.'

Sayber lowers into the seat behind him and gestures for Bray to join him. 'You know who I am, right?'

'Sure, that's why you need someone to watch your back. From what I heard in Tyrat, you've got an impressive target plastered on it.'

Sayber grunts. 'You could say that.' He narrows his eyes. 'You look familiar. I know you from somewhere?'

Bray shrugs. 'I've been in Tyrat for a few years. Can't see how.'

Sayber grunts again and shakes his head. He stands up and gestures for his men to follow him. Bray's breath freezes in his chest as the group climb down the steps. He blew it. Bray glances over at Avoca and sees the same worry on his face. Bray's mind races, trying to come up with something he can do or say to convince Sayber to take him back to his ship.

He yelps as Sayber's face appears in front of him out of nowhere. 'Well, I ain't got all day to wait for you. Move your arse.'

Bray only manages a nod as he tries to control his racing heart. He hurries after the tall Hunter. Before he turns the corner he glances over his shoulder. Avoca smiles and nods. He's done it.

PART 3

2 YEARS LATER

GRYFFIN – 32 YEARS OLD
BRAY – 27 YEARS OLD

ULTAR

Aleena stares at the small screen on her desk in disbelief. The three words rouse a flood of emotions - some good, but most not so.

'Permission to land.'

At least Gryffin was asking - something she doubts he is well known for. That does not mean she will grant his request. Two years have passed since he left in the middle of the night without so much as an explanation. Her feelings about the situation have not wavered in that time. If anything, she has grown more irritated and... well, furious at the Nomad. Not just Gryffin, but the whole group. The way they operate, their chain of command, their unwavering loyalty to that brute Rayde. The entire thing makes her want to scream. In all her years as a leader, she has never felt this way, and until she meets with Gryffin face to face, she will never dispel those unwanted feelings. Perhaps screaming at him will help.

Her hand hovers over the reply button. Rayde had made his dislike of her known. Would he have sent his favourite mercenary to Ultar to kill her? She shakes her head. Trading is a lucrative business - for both the Ultarans and the Nomad. She very much doubts even Rayde would be so foolish. So why the unexpected visit after so long? There is only one way she is going to find out. She pauses for another minute before she finally gives her approval.

She watches as the screen shows *Ares* has received her message, then shuts it off and pushes it to the back of her desk. Usually, she would go meet Gryffin, but not today. Instead, she prepares herself a cup of tea and takes it outside. She sits on the wooden bench in her garden and waits to see what he will do.

She had expected him to return a long time ago, but yet again, he had proved her wrong. Perhaps his stubbornness had kept him away. Perhaps it was shame at his actions. Perhaps it was nothing more complex than an order from Rayde. Whatever the reason, *Ares* had not returned until now. Many other Nomad vessels had traded in her place - something that only served to irk her more.

Initially she believed he was avoiding all contact

with the colonies, but when she heard from some of her acquaintances that he had been to their worlds, she knew without a doubt that he was avoiding Ultar. And her.

She closes her eyes and listens to the birds in the trees surrounding her house. She's excited about possibly seeing him again, and that irritates her. Curiosity is winning over everything else. Why, after two quiet years, had he decided to come back now?

About fifteen minutes later she hears the distant rumble of a powerful engine. The motorcycle comes to a stop in front of her house. She glances up at the machine and its rider. Nomad deals must be proving lucrative if he can afford a machine like that. She waits for more vehicles to emerge from the trees but he appears to be alone. Perhaps he does not wish for anyone to witness whatever is about to happen. She moves her attention back to her tea as the rider dismounts. The gravel on the path leading to her house crunches under his boots as he walks towards her.

She sips her tea and keeps her attention on the insects swarming around her flowers. He stops beside her, casting a long shadow over her garden. 'Can I sit?'

'You may, but over there.' She nods at the seat under the tree facing hers. He pauses briefly then sits down. Aleena risks a quick look at him. Gryffin's attention is on the flowers so her examination stretches on a little longer. The first thing that hits her is how much she missed him. The Nomad appears so much bigger than she remembers. He's leaning forward, his arms resting on his legs and his gloved hands clasped tightly together. His dark hair is hiding his face as usual, but he appears well enough and very much alive. Something she is thankful for. After the way he left the last time and Rayde's decision to medicate him, a part of her had been expecting the worst. He does seem a little unsure of how to act and so he should.

'Didn't think you'd let *Ares* land.'

Thanks to the injury to his neck his voice is deeper and huskier. Not altogether unpleasant and, she must admit, it suits him. 'I was in two minds, but I admit I was curious. You disappear in the middle of the night without an explanation, then wait two years before making contact again. Two years is a long time, Captain. I am surprised you could remember where my house was.'

'I get you're angry. About the last time. I didn't mean to...'

'Throw me against the wall and pin me by my neck. What is there to be angry about?'

She looks over at him to see his reaction. His head drops lower, his shoulders hunched as he examines the gravel between his boots. 'I'm sorry, Aleena.'

To hide her shock, Aleena takes another sip of her tea. 'I appreciate you saying that. So, Captain, what did he give you?'

Gryffin lifts his head and his dark blue eyes meet hers. Time has done nothing to diminish his looks. If anything, the Nomad captain is improving with age.

'Do not look at me like that. You know what I am referring to. Rayde kindly left the pressure syringe on your bed, so do not lie to me. I believe it is the least I deserve. Answer me, Captain, or you can take your ship and leave here for another two years.'

He looks towards her house then back at her. 'A stimulant. Something to keep me on my feet until I faced the crew. If I showed weakness after what happened it would undermine my position as Captain.'

Well, wonders never cease. She was not expecting an answer. She also had no idea how she could force him to leave Ultar had he not responded. 'Did it work?'

'I'm High Commander.'

Aleena stares at him open-mouthed. Even though she is still upset at what he did, she cannot help but be pleased for him. Reaching the most esteemed position in the Nomad group at such a young age is quite an achievement. 'Congratulations, Gryffin. That is impressive. Can I ask if the former High Commander is still with us?'

'I didn't kill Rayde if that's what you're asking. I wasn't planning on challenging his position. I was happy being Captain, but the group wanted me in charge. Some of the other Captains told him how they felt. Rayde stepped down and I was made High Commander.'

'I cannot imagine he was overly happy about that decision.'

Gryffin smirks. 'You met him. What do you think?'

Aleena only met him once but she has no doubt he was less than pleased to be unseated by Gryffin. 'So, it was all worth it.'

'Not what I did to you. The stimulant messed with my implants. It triggered the one in my head. I should have kept better control of it, but I wasn't strong enough. I would never hurt you, Aleena. You know that, don't you?'

'Not at the time.' She looks him in the eye. 'You scared me, Gryffin.'

He looks away again and takes a deep breath, but doesn't say anything. There is not a lot he can say.

'Has your new promotion prompted the timing for this visit.'

'I don't have to justify my actions anymore. Gives me more freedom.'

'So Rayde ordered you to stay away.'

'My command was in question. I had to concentrate on that.'

'I take that as a yes. Why did you leave without speaking to me? Can I presume that was also under Rayde's orders?'

'I needed to be seen in command of *Ares*. I also wanted to get Rayde off Ultar. Didn't feel right him being here.' He pauses and frowns. 'What?'

'Excuse me?'

'Your face changed when I mentioned getting him off Ultar. You got a problem with him?'

'Not a problem as such. I...' she pauses, unable to voice her feelings.

'You what?'

'I did not warm to the man. My initial feelings were reinforced when he gave you drugs which could have impeded your recovery. It was a reckless and foolish thing to do. Was that the first time? I fear I already know the response but I would very much like to hear it from you.'

His face hardens. 'I don't question how you run Ultar.'

'This is different.'

'No, it's not. Don't push me, Aleena.'

'Very well.' His refusal to answer is all the answer she needs. Perhaps with Rayde's removal as High Commander, the practice would cease.

'I'll keep him away from here. Your deal has always been with *Ares*. Now it's with the Nomad fleet commanded by me. You don't want him here, I'll make sure that happens.'

'I appreciate that.'

'Rayde's been good to me, but he can be difficult. He's respected but not liked by many Nomad.'

'I cannot think why,' she adds with a grin.

Gryffin smiles at her and looks back to the flowers. 'I can assign another ship to deal with you if you want.'

She pauses to drink her tea again then shakes her head. 'I would be doing the Ultarans I lead a disservice by letting this incident undo everything we have worked for. But I will say one thing, High Commander. You will not behave like that with me again. Do I make myself clear?'

He meets her eyes again. 'Understood.'

ULTAR

Gryffin focuses on the view of Aleena's garden out the window. Once things had been smoothed out with Aleena, he had released the rest of his crew. Keeping away from Ultar had been difficult on his men. Ultar was the one place off *Ares* they could be themselves. The one place they could relax and mingle with other people. The time away had taken a toll on all of them - himself included. He didn't realise until he saw her how much he had missed Aleena.

If he thought for one second the stimulant would trigger his control implant he would have... would have what? Told Rayde no? That wasn't an option. He closes his eyes and forces the memories away. It's done now. Aleena has let the Nomad back on Ultar and he's in charge of the fleet. Shame had played a part in keeping him from Ultar but time is against him now.

He looks down at the badge on the front of his jacket. Being made Captain was honour enough. High Commander was a rank he never aspired to. Then Rayde announced he was stepping down and the group backed his nomination. After the failed mutiny, having over two hundred Nomad across ten ships back him was a welcome surprise. The way he dealt with the mutiny and his speedy return to command after had solidified his reputation. Something he has to thank Rayde for.

Aleena places a glass of water on the table and pats the couch beside her. 'Have a seat. What did you want to speak to me about?'

He pulls off his jacket and sits beside her. 'Have I killed any trust there was between us.'

Aleena peers into her drink then places the cup on the table and looks up at him. 'No. Damaged it perhaps, but nothing that cannot be repaired. You would not have been permitted to land otherwise. Not that I could have stopped you.'

'I told you a while ago that I distrust you less than most people I deal with.'

She smiles and nods. 'Yes, a truly memorable compliment.'

'I trust you, Aleena. Haven't said that to anyone before.'

'Thank you, Gryffin. That means a lot.

'What I'm about to ask you, I'm only asking because I trust you. I need you to know that.'

'I am listening.'

'I want to build a ship. On Ultar.'

She quietly looks at him, her face losing all signs of emotion. 'A ship.'

'In the tunnels.'

'I see. Is this what you had planned all along? Is this agreement in place so you could eventually take over the colony and make it a Nomad world? I should have known you came back for a reason.'

He shakes his head. 'No. I'm not planning on taking Ultar. This has nothing to do with the Nomad. Like I said, this deal is between us. Just you and me.'

She blinks rapidly a few times before she answers. 'I can honestly say I was not expecting this. Forgive me, but why would you - apologies - we, build a ship?'

'We'll need it.'

'That answers all my questions. Thank you.' Her sarcasm isn't lost on him. 'You will need to be a little more articulate if I am going to continue this conversation. Tell me why we need a ship of all things.'

'I was designed to be a weapon, Aleena. There's no other reason I would have been altered like this. Someone put a lot of time and credits into me. They'll come looking for me.'

'A weapon?'

'The Nomad don't fully understand what my implants do. All I know is that the control implant in my brain was put there for a reason. When it takes over, I can't stop it. I just react and take down anyone near me. It doesn't care if I'm facing an ally or an enemy. You saw that first hand. Once it's out... I can't get it back in easily. I'm keeping it under control most of the time, but I don't know if that'll last.'

'So you would intend to use this new ship to protect you from your... creators for want of a better word.'

'No. It would be used to protect the Sector from me.'

She stares at him in shocked silence for a moment. 'Am I understanding this correctly? You want me to build a ship that can destroy you.' He nods. 'I am not going to be involved in building a ship whose sole purpose is to destroy you. Even if I do agree - which I am far from doing - we cannot build a ship on Ultar. We have no parts. We have no knowledge. We will need serious assistance from you.'

'I have a ship we've begun working on. It's in an old mine on another colony, but I don't want to leave it there. I don't trust it won't be found. I want to move it here along with the team. I can pay you to work on it, send as many people as you need, but that's all I can do. If my creators - when my creators get me, they could be able to access everything I know. There's a chip in my head. Who knows what information is being stored in there. I can't know anything about this. You'll need to organise it all.'

'I am almost afraid to ask where you obtained a ship from.'

'Don't ask then. It's not suitable as it is, but it'll give you something to work on. I can have it delivered in a few days. If you agree of course.'

'This is quite a request, Gryffin. Is this the reason you asked for the tunnels to remain hidden? Have you been planning this since the first time you were down there?'

'Yes. I need your help, Aleena. Whoever did this to me will have a lot of credits and damn all conscience. The guards in Tyrat will have reported that I have a metal arm and other implants. It's only a matter of time before that information gets to the wrong ears. I want something in place when that happens.'

'I do not know where to start.'

Gryffin digs in his jacket pocket and hands a small unit to her. 'I've run a background check on some of your colonists - just the ones not born on Ultar. There are five names on the list with previous experience. A lot of your people have past lives. You'd be surprised how much experience you have on the surface. I'll move crew around my ships, free up men to work with you, but I can't do it at once or it'll be noticed.'

She looks at the list. 'Saul, Lucan, Reece, Alder, and Callon? These men recently relocated to Ultar from a neighbouring colony. Are you sure?'

'Yes. You'll need all the help you can get. Only people you trust. Understood?'

'I understand.' She blows out a long breath. 'I did not think this day would turn out like this. I thought you arriving at my door was bad enough. I was prepared for an argument. Or at least for some therapeutic shouting. This... this is difficult to get my head around.'

'Shout at me if it helps.'

'I believe this request is far beyond a mere shout.'

'I know I'm asking a lot.'

'That is a great understatement.' She places the list on the table in front of her and chews her bottom lip as she stares ahead of her. 'Surely there is another option. Something else that can be done to prevent whatever you think is coming.'

'Having a ship to protect the Sector is the best thing I can come up with. This isn't just about protecting you from me. You need protection from whoever they are. The Nomad will step up but that might not be enough. I'll bring more ships to my side if I can, but this could be what tips the balance in your favour.'

'But if you are captured, what then? Are your Nomad to use this ship to... kill you?'

He shrugs. 'I don't know what I was created for. If I'm being used to hurt people, yes.'

'There must be another way, Gryffin.'

He pulls his battered gun out of its holster and places it on the table in front of her. 'You've seen me try the alternative. My programming won't let me do it.'

'Will not let you? Are you saying if it did let you...' She pauses and looks up at him. 'Please say you are not asking me to-'

'Never. Besides, I need to hang around to make sure

you have everything you need to get this ship off the ground. Can't do it without you though.'

Her eyes move from him to the gun, lying on the table. 'I need to consider this. I will give you my answer later today.'

'I'll be on *Ares*.'

He pulls his jacket off the chair, leaves and mounts his bike. He wasn't expecting an instant yes from Aleena. A part of him wasn't expecting a yes at all. He enters his code starting the engine, then follows the path through the trees back to *Ares*. He pulls the bike to a stop at the lake and cuts the engine. He massages the thick scar across his neck. What he initially saw as a reminder of a failing, he now sees as a second chance. He survived the mutiny and came out with this head attached.

The Nomad put their trust in him again, and there was no fucking way he would let them down. That's why this ship is such a priority.

He turns in his saddle as the horse-drawn cart bumps along the path behind him. In the back are the five refugees he highlighted to Aleena. She must be checking into the men before she makes any decisions. That's better than an outright no.

From this distance and with his jacket on he doesn't stand out from any of the other Nomad on the planet. Since their relationship has developed, his men had taken to leaving their masks off in the town. It was one of the few places they were truly safe. If she's going to be taking in new colonists every few weeks he may have to rethink that rule.

The five men turn in their seats at the sight of a Nomad. One by one, they quickly look anywhere else but at him. Except for one. A tall, dark-haired man at the back meets his eyes and holds them.

It took longer than planned for Lucan to get to Ultar. Aleena will never know he was put on Ultar by Gryffin, or that he'd be Gryffin's eyes and ears on the surface. Aleena may not spot a threat until it's too late, but Lucan's years of Nomad training will be invaluable – for the safety of the Ultarans and the new ship. All he needs is Aleena to say yes to his plan so Lucan can do his job.

Gryffin straightens in his saddle and Lucan finally retreats under his glare. Gryffin knows Lucan will do everything he can to convince Aleena he can help her. Having him on the surface gives Gryffin a little comfort, but not much. Something is coming and he's got no damn idea what it is. How the fuck do you prepare to meet an enemy you don't know anything about? He could build a dozen ships and it still not be enough.

'Sir?'

He jumps slightly as Klay approaches. 'What?'

'You okay?'

'Yeah. What is it?'

'We've checked the defences. No mistaking who's got Ultar under their wing. Anyone pushes that they know the Nomad will come after them. I need to check your implants while we're here.'

'Give me ten minutes.'

Klay nods and disappears into the trees. Gryffin looks over his shoulder, barely able to make out the details of the cart as it rattles along the dirt path.

46

Gryffin pulls into the clearing and shuts the engine off. He swings his leg over the saddle and leans against the bike as he waits for the others to arrive. Chayse appears first, picking his way through the undergrowth. In the two years since he joined the crew, Gryffin had done what he planned on doing when he decided to take him on - wiped the smile off his face. His new aide did everything that was asked of him without question and was proving himself. He doesn't want to admit it, but since Chayse has been on board, he's had a lot more time away from his desk.

Kellyn and Desyl had taken to training him, building the frail young man into a fighter. Good meals and regular training had added bulk to his wiry frame. His first Nomad tattoo decorated one arm. If he keeps going the way he is, he can get the other arm done in a few weeks. If he survived that long.

He may be proving himself, but he isn't trusted among the other Nomad. He's too close to Gryffin. The crew was careful to watch what they said when he was near. Couldn't have him running to tell the captain all their dirty little secrets.

Not that Gryffin could give a fuck about anything the crew are saying behind his back. All he wants is respect. What did it matter if the crew thought he was a bastard or the sweetest guy on the ship? He'd be a shit Captain if he kicked someone off the crew for not liking him. As long as the men followed orders and respected his command, they were part of the crew.

Didn't help Chayse, but that was his problem. Gryffin didn't share meals with anyone. He didn't drink or chat with anyone. Didn't do him any harm. Wouldn't do Chayse any harm either. If anything, it would toughen him up.

'Aleena with you?'

Chayse nods and gestures behind him as Aleena steps into the clearing.

'Didn't think you'd want to talk so soon. You followed?'

She shakes her head. 'I do not believe so.'

'Chayse?'

'I checked. It's just the three of us. Sir, the locater on your bike-'

'Dismantled.' He holds out two pieces of metal still covered with blood. 'Took the one from behind my ear and broke it. We're clear.'

Chayse and Aleena stare at the bloody pieces of metal in his hand. He meant to wipe the blood off but forgot. Too late now. The monitoring device took a bit of digging to remove from his skin. He'll get Chayse to fit a new one when they get back to the ship.

'Chayse. Stay with my bike. Contact me if you see or hear anyone coming. Understood?'

'Yes, sir.'

His aide walks over to the bike and leans on the seat before a stern glare from Gryffin has him on his feet again.

'He is a pleasant young man.'

Gryffin grunts at Aleena as they walk towards the entrance of the cave. 'He'll do.'

She reaches for him and he ducks out of the way. 'Stand still for a moment. There is blood dribbling down your neck. Why did you do that to yourself?'

'Just leave it.' He pulls his gun out as he checks the inside of the cave. 'What the hell are you laughing at?'

Aleena shakes her head as she walks further into the cave. 'You. Are you expecting a bat to attack you?'

He opens the door to the mine and walks in silence towards the vast cavern. He glances over at the cage resting in the corner. Hopefully, he doesn't end up in there again. He signals Chayse. 'You read me?'

'Yes, sir.'

'We good?'

'Yes, sir.'

'You sitting on my bike?'

A rustle of leather is followed by a quick. 'No, sir.'

Gryffin curses under his breath then turns to face Aleena. 'Made a decision?'

She sits on a crate of mining supplies and looks around the cavern. 'You do know what you are asking. Have you truly looked at this place? It is a shell. How can you envision it being a suitable facility for building a ship?'

'It's doable.'

'How exactly? If you do send us this carcass to work on, and if we do manage to somehow hide it in here - what then? Where do we even begin? We are in an abandoned mine.'

'I'll sort it all out.'

'Oh, it is that simple?'

'If you agree, in less than a month I can have men in place, machinery, parts, generators, whatever you need.'

She eyes him suspiciously. 'I know you have brokered deals with quite a few colonies, but I did not realise they were such affluent ones.'

Gryffin doesn't answer. She won't like it if he does.

'Are you stealing it?'

'No.'

'You mean to tell me you are paying for the equipment?'

'Yes.'

'Where are you getting the credits?'

'What the hell does that have to do with anything?' She walks towards the entrance. 'Wait.'

'I believe I have seen you at your worst. Tell me or this ends now.'

If he has this conversation with her, it'll spell the end of this ship seeing the light of day. 'We're taking more mercenary work.'

'I see. Do you mean we or you.'

'Me.'

'What manner of work do you undertake?'

'Anything - as long as it pays well. Aleena, running the fleet is expensive. The defences I'm setting up around colonies are expensive. We're trading but we still need to supply food and medical supplies to some of the harder hit colonies. This ship... it's going to need a hell of a lot of credits to get off the ground. Unless I'm going to bring the Nomad back to where they were, taking whatever the hell we want from whoever has it, I have to do something to get us the extra credits.'

'Do you... would you take a life?'

'Yes.'

'I see,' she says again. He's been around her enough to know she's less than happy when she uses those two words. 'Is this ship worth killing over?'

'Yes.'

She gets up and walks around the cavern, lost in her thoughts. Gryffin rests his hand on his gun, half hoping someone interrupts so he can get out of this conversation. She's going to say no. What he just said would have tipped the scales as far from a yes as it could go. Recent actions haven't gone a long way to solidify any trust she may have had in him. He's keeping them safe, but thanks to what's happened lately, he's proved himself as much of a threat as anyone he's trying to stop.

Maybe it's time to change that. She needs to see exactly what they're up against.

He stands up and pulls off his gloves, jacket, and shirt. He takes his guns and knife out of their holsters and lays them on top of his coat, then pulls the bandanna out of his pocket, tying it around his head to keep his hair off his face. Before he changes his mind, he takes hold of his metal arm and twists his elbow out of the housing. He places the prosthetic next to his weapons and turns around to face her, feeling more naked than he actually is.

'What are you doing?'

'My left eye is artificial,' he says, desperate to get the words out before he changes his mind. 'It's meant to be a hi-tech replacement but it's not reliable. I can't see clearly - everything's blurred unless I'm using the control implant in my head. The metal round my eye is screwed to my skull. It links with the control implant on or in my brain. When everything is working together, it improves my vision. I can see clearer, further and in the dark.' He laughs harshly. 'Has its uses I guess. Most of my organs have implants attached to them. They keep my body operating at its peak. They all link with this piece on my chest.' He points to one of the many connectors along the metalwork. 'These connectors allow access to my internal implants. That's how Kellyn could stabilise my heart after Sayber attacked me. I can be plugged into a computer so every detail of my body can be examined and analysed and monitored like a damn drone. The technology is good, but it's far from perfect. The implants fail from time to time. Chayse, Kellyn, and Klay know how to reboot my implants if something goes wrong. I can survive for a short time without them, but my body is too dependent on them to last longer than a few minutes. I can't get them removed either. They go and I die.'

He swallows and holds up his right arm. 'The Scientist used a rusted saw to cut off my hand. He never treated any of the wounds when he was done so it got infected. He eventually removed the infected part and embedded a series of connectors to my bone. Guess he got bored after that. He never fitted the lower arm – just left me with the connectors and nothing else. When the Nomad found me the wound was infected again, so I had to lose more of my arm before they could finally give me the prosthetic.

'Everything was done to me while I was conscious. I could feel every cut. I could feel every implant being fitted. Feel every screw being drilled in place. If I lost consciousness, I'd be revived and he'd continue. It was like he was doing everything he could to hurt me. He used to smile when I...' Gryffin's voice trails away as he remembers the particular smile his tormentor reserved for him.

He'll probably never know why he received such different treatment to the others, but whatever the reason, he's convinced it was personal. The Scientist took too much pleasure from hearing him suffer. He put too much effort into hurting him in as many elaborate ways as possible. You don't do that unless you want revenge or payback for something. If he ever got his hands on The Scientist, he sure as hell would take his time repaying the favour.

He tears himself away from the image of the bastard, broken and bleeding as he begs Gryffin for his life. He just hopes The Scientist is still alive and he gets his chance to kill him one day.

He takes a breath and continues. 'The people who did this to me did it to other children too. I can't sleep because every time I close my eyes I see them being hurt. I hear them screaming. I see them dying.

'I was tortured every single day for years. I've lost parts of myself I'll never get back. I've seen pieces of me being removed and thrown on the floor.'

Aleena's face loses all trace of colour as she slumps to the ground. 'Gryffin... please...'

He crouches down in front of her and lets the control implant out, turning his eyes purple. 'I need you to look at me. Really look at me. At the implants. At the screws. At the scars.'

'Gryffin-'

'Please, Aleena.' She lifts her head and examines the parts of himself he's ashamed of. 'I didn't ask for any of this to be done to me. I'm damn sure I didn't do anything to deserve it. I know I was the only survivor on that station but I don't know how many more locations there were. I don't know if there's someone else out there like me. There could be ten more. A hundred. All I know is that this was done to me for a reason. Most of it was just to hurt me, but the implant in my head is different. Something in there takes control of me and there's nothing I can do about it. That scares the hell out of me. We may never need this ship. I hope whoever created me won't come back. I hope they're rotting in the fucking ground, but I can't take that risk. I need to have something in place and if I have to kill for credits to pay for it, I'll do it.'

He closes his eyes and takes hold of the implant before he looks at her again. 'You may not like what I do, what I am, but whoever did this to me has no problem torturing kids. I've done a lot of things you wouldn't like and I'm going to keep doing them. It's who I am, but I hope by now you also know I would never stoop that low. The Nomad are the closest thing I have to a family and I will do whatever I can to protect the group. That also goes for the colonies I protect.

'If this ship can be used to defend the Nomad and the colonies from whoever these people are - can protect you from me - I have to make sure it happens. I'm not going to push you on this. You say no, I'll figure something else out.' If she says no they're fucked.

He freezes as Aleena throws her arms around his neck and holds him close. She pulls away and smiles apologetically. 'I am sorry, Gryffin. I did not mean to do that. I hope I have not upset you.'

'Why are you crying?'

She wipes her face, trying to dry the tears. 'I am not going to dignify that with a response.'

'I didn't tell you that to make you cry. I just needed you to understand what these people are like. Why I need to do this.'

She sniffs and wipes her eyes. 'Oh, you have made me understand. It was as subtle as being struck by a cart but quite effective.' She casts her eyes over his arm and smiles sadly. 'I also understand why the Nomad are so important to you. Even Rayde.'

'They saved my life.'

She hugs her knees to her chest and looks around the cavern. He doesn't push her for an answer. He's thrown enough information at her over the last few minutes. She'll need time to get her head around it.

'Very well, Gryffin.'

'What?' He wasn't expecting an answer so soon.

'That was a yes. I still do not comprehend how it will be done but you can build your ship here. I for one would not welcome a visit from whoever hurt you. I also hope for their sake they do not attempt to find you.'

He agrees with her on that last point. Gryffin helps her to her feet and goes back to his things. He passes Aleena his arm. 'It's awkward to line up the connectors. Can you hold it out?' She adjusts the angle until everything is where is should be, then holds it steady while he slips it back on and locks the connectors in place. He gets dressed and contacts Chayse. 'We still clear?'

'Yes, sir.'

'I'm on my way back.'

He slips his guns back in place and pulls the bandanna off his head. 'I'll get the ship sent in a few days.'

'Very well. I have spoken to the men you recommended. I agree they are promising. I especially like the one called Lucan. He is very pleasant.'

Gryffin nods. Not a bad start. 'I'll be leaving in a few hours. I want us off the surface before the ship arrives.'

'I understand.'

They step outside and he squints as the sun hits his messed up eyes. 'I won't be able to source everything you need without someone noticing. I'll send credits whenever I can. With those five helping you, you should be able to source anything I can't.'

'You are placing a lot of trust in me, Captain - both with this matter and what you told me in the cavern.'

He shrugs. 'This won't work unless we trust each other. Too much to lose on both sides.' They enter the clearing and Chayse stands to attention - far away from his bike. 'Make sure Aleena gets back to the village in one piece. I'll be there in a bit. I'll need you to fit the new tracker to me.'

'Yes, sir,'

Chayse walks away with Aleena, quickly disappearing into the trees.

KRATOS

Rayde lowers into the massive, high-backed, leather-covered chair, and sighs. His initial regrets at handing over *Ares* to Gryffin had quickly faded away after a few days on *Kratos*. The vessel is smaller than the flagship but far more modern. For starters, everything works. The extra credits brought in by Gryffin's trade deals has helped to furnish his quarters in a manner he never thought possible. He's not going to admit trading is the way to go, but he's certainly not going to refuse his cut.

He pulls the latest report from *Ares* from the top of the pile. Another four colonies have signed up. He sighs again and throws the file back on his desk. He's losing his grip on the group. Losing the respect of the men he used to lead. Compared to Gryffin, he wasn't bringing anything of value to the Nomad. His years of graft, dragging the group from the bottom of the food chain was rapidly being overshadowed by Gryffin's deals.

He takes his dagger from his belt and examines the polished blade. He can still see traces of Gryffin's blood where the blade meets the hilt. The weight of his mistake threatens to crush him. None of this was meant to happen.

Initially, his intentions went no further than rescuing a boy desperately in need of help. Things shouldn't have changed when he realised how powerful the boy could be - but they did. He's not ashamed of that. Life in the Outer Sector is a constant battle. Finding you have a weapon on your ship would have got anyone thinking of the possibilities.

It's just a shame the weapon began to think for itself.

He can't quite put his finger on when things began to change between them. Perhaps the signs had been there all along but he refused to see the truth. Gryffin had found the courage to question him one too many times. He should have put him back in his place with a little more force. Trained him a little longer. Cut him a little deeper. Beat him a little harder. Maybe if he did, the ungrateful bastard wouldn't be prancing around the Sector in his ship with his group looking to him like he's some sort of fucking hero.

Stepping down from *Ares* had cut him to his core, but he had no choice. Instead of seeing him as a threat, the Nomad saw Gryffin as their saviour. With the credits pouring in it was hard to argue against that fact. It was either step down and give him *Ares* or be unseated by force.

Giving him the High Commander position wasn't by choice either but better to go willingly than be forced out. At least if he stepped down while still in favour with Gryffin he could keep a little hold on what the boy was doing. It's the only option he has left. He's tried everything else.

When Creed had asked one too many questions, sending Gryffin to deal with him was the obvious choice. While he waited on the command deck, Rayde had told the crew Gryffin was going to have a word with the commander. They didn't need to know he had ordered the boy to kill Creed. It had gone better than he planned. Instead of merely killing Creed, he had spaced him. Rayde had barely managed to contain himself. Unfortunately, his crew's reaction to Gryffin's deed had also not gone to plan. By labelling Creed a traitor they expected he'd be killed. That one had backfired and he lost a good member of the crew for nothing.

He grabs the jug of ale off his desk and takes a large mouthful. It was after that he decided there was little choice but to kill Gryffin. Unfortunately, as with every other plan he drafted, killing the boy was proving a great deal harder than he thought it would be.

Giving him up to the Slavers when he went to trade with the Arta Brothers didn't work either. He had sent the Nomad who had the most issues with the new addition. They were all meant to be captured by the Slavers or Gryffin was meant to lose control and kill the men. He didn't really care which one. Either way, he would have fixed the problem.

Instead, Gryffin had somehow saved them all. Bringing back a new ship, sacks of weapons and more credits than they would've raised in a year had been yet more knives in Rayde's back. Rayde still can't quite figure out what the hell happened on the surface. All he knows is that Gryffin earned himself some new fans that day.

He was sure he was on to a winner when he instigated his arrest and imprisonment on Tyrat. The prison is notorious for being the one place in the Sector truly secure. No one had escaped. No one except fucking Gryffin. If anything, he'd come out the other end with his reputation as a lethal killer and ferocious fighter solidified. At least he was able to convince Gryffin to kill Rafe before the man could point the finger at him. Not that he could. Rayde had never met the man nor given him his name. Nevertheless, it was a loose end that wouldn't come back to bite him.

He takes another drink, savouring the heat as the liquid moves down his throat. He's running out of options. That stunt by Gryffin has only solidified his place in the group. Damn knows he tried but he was powerless to keep the news about his escape a secret. Within days, most of the Sector knew. Although he can't help but be a little impressed he survived the interrogation and managed to escape with a broken arm among other injuries. No doubt thanks to the intensive training Rayde gave him. If one more Nomad captain got in contact with Rayde to quiz him about his new protégé he was quite likely to lose his cool

Rayde stares into the murky liquid in his glass. No, he'll just have to bide his time. He created Gryffin. The Nomad he is today is down to Rayde's time and effort. He'll figure out a way to bring him down and put him back in his place as Rayde's enforcer. At least with Klay in place, he had eyes and ears on *Ares*. Gryffin had let his guard down there. His confidence had been temporarily knocked by Sayber and Rayde was only too happy to take advantage.

He leans back in the chair paid for by Gryffin and smiles to himself. Let the boy have some fun while he can. He does deserve it after whatever hell he went through in the lab. Besides, having the Nomad flying as one unit may not be the worst thing Gryffin did. At least, when Rayde takes over again, he'll have a powerful fleet under his command.

Rayde sips his drink, pondering his predicament. If only there was a way of finding out who modified him in the first place. If Rayde could somehow find out why he was altered the way he was, he could harness Gryffin, use him to make the Nomad truly formidable again. He smiles to himself. They spent all that time and effort removing the metal, helping to bring him back from the brink of whatever hell he was in. How ironic would it be if the boy ended up in precisely the same position he started, but this time with Rayde organising the process. That would put the boy firmly back in his place. Rayde will take back what's his - it's only a matter of time.

PART 4

1 YEAR LATER

GRYFFIN – 33 YEARS OLD

BRAY – 28 YEARS OLD

(BACK IN THE 'PRESENT' DAY AT THE

BEGINNING OF *ARES* (BOOK 1)

ARES

'Captain, we're nearing the location of the unidentified signal.'

Gryffin ignores his radio as he focuses on the training drone in front of him. The life-sized robot circles him, patiently waiting for his next move. Gryffin twirls the sparring stick in his metal hand. Another message sounds over the intercom, calling him to the command deck. So much for a few hours of peace and quiet.

With no time left for a proper fight, he launches himself at the drone. He dodges a swipe to the head and ducks under the drone's arm. Swinging around, he swipes the machine across its side. It retaliates by striking Gryffin squarely on the metal implant fused to his chest. He grunts in pain and withdraws for a few seconds. The drone relaxes slightly. Gryffin takes advantage and fakes right. When the drone reacts, he jams his sparring stick into its side. Sparks of electricity spit from the wound before the drone collapses to the floor.

Gryffin holds the drone down with his foot and yanks his stick from the machine. After placing it back on the rack against the wall, he drags the drone to the corner and dumps it with the other scrap. He grabs his t-shirt from the bench and climbs the spiral metal staircase to the upper level.

The crew members he meets on his way to the command deck stand to attention as he storms past. As he walks, he glances down at his chest. The damn drone's lucky hit tore the skin joined to the W-shaped metal implant framing his chest. He ignores the wound and pulls on his t-shirt as he gets to his destination.

The command deck falls silent when he enters. 'What have you got?'

'Take a look for yourself, sir.' His first officer, Klay, steps aside to give the captain an unobstructed view of the ship in front of them. The sleek silver vessel is clearly a long distance cruiser. A ship of that calibre so far from the border can only mean trouble. He clenches his jaw and digs his metal hand into the console in front of him.

'Foundation ship?'

Klay nods soberly. 'Confirmed.'

Klay steps back as the metal surrounding Gryffin's left eye glows deep purple. 'So, the Foundation has officially arrived in the Sector. Greedy bastards must want to colonise.'

'I can't think of any other reason for them to be here, sir.'

Gryffin sits back in his command chair and quietly surveys the Foundation ship. He had heard rumours they'd entered the Sector, but this is the first time he's seen them in the flesh. He's vaguely aware of his crew moving at their stations around him. They're waiting for the order to strike. They've taken down bigger ships and he's sure they can overcome this vessel.

'Do you want to launch an attack, sir?'

'Not yet. Let them make the first move. Bring us closer to the ship.' The scarred battleship slowly manoeuvres into position behind the larger Foundation vessel. With cloaks engaged, *Ares* can approach the Foundation without alerting them to her presence.

Gryffin doesn't have to wait long for the stern of the ship to open. He leans back in his chair and watches three small transports exit the cargo hatch of the Foundation vessel, unaware of their audience.

They're heading towards the surface of the planet.

So it's beginning — they've chosen their first colony to target. He smiles to himself. It's just their bad luck they decided to start with one of his. As soon as they step foot on the planet, their fate will be sealed. While a part of him hopes they'll abort, he's itching for them to land. It's been too long since he's had a proper fight. Time seems to slow for him as the three ships on the screen move closer to the world. His purple eyes glow in anticipation of the upcoming battle. He rises to his feet. 'Ready the raiding teams. Time to go introduce ourselves.'

PERSES

'Do you know how much shit I'll be in if they find out we've been talking?' Bray hisses at the screen.

The video feed blurs as the connection fights to get through the vast number of satellites it's being shunted around. Avoca's mouth opens but no sound comes out.

'The connection is terrible. Say that again?'

'They know he's alive.'

Bray stares at the screen as the information sinks in. 'Have you got confirmation?'

'I was just at a meeting. We're coming after him. Are you ready?'

'I guess.'

'That reply is not filling me with confidence, Bray. You need to be sure.'

'You know the odds of the Foundation getting their hands on him is not worth mentioning. It's not going to happen. I know of at least a dozen attempts to capture or kill him and no one's come close. I'm damn sure the people after him in this Sector are a hell of a lot more experienced than the Foundation.'

'Things are different now. There is too much at stake. Balfe will send Foundation ships and also utilise parties already in the Sector. I would be highly surprised if Sayber is not contacted shortly. He may already have been spoken to. He is known to us and would be the obvious choice. Balfe will work with the devil himself if it means finishing the project. If that doesn't happen, Gryffin will be killed. Leaving him alive is far too much of a risk. Can you imagine if the truth got out? They stole children and did...' he pauses and looks away from the screen. 'Balfe will do whatever he has to in order to keep the truth away from the population. They speak of continuing the work but I fear he will be killed if that is not possible.'

'After what they did to him that's probably the better option.'

'He needs to live and you need to ensure that happens. It's important.'

Bray carefully examines the admiral's face as he speaks. 'There's something you're not telling me.'

'I've told you all I can, Bray. Please.'

'Right. Fine. I'll be ready.'

'That's good.' Avoca cuts the connection leaving Bray staring at a blank screen. He sighs and runs a hand through his hair, ruffling the soft spikes. He brings up the schematics for the mod he designed and checks the details again. Without direct access to the Nomad leader, a lot of the design is based off old schematics Avoca gave him. Most of that is guessing too. Avoca wasn't there when the control implant was fitted so he has no idea if any alterations were made. The whole plan is based firmly on speculation. Not a great start. Bray doesn't care though.

Thanks to Avoca and the Dixon's he's finally found himself a home. *Perses* may be a little on the unreliable side. Sayber may be a little on the crazy side, but Bray is part of the team. Part of the family. That's something he hasn't felt for a hell of a long time. Since Daegan died, he's lost control of his life - even from a young age. He was fighting a ghost his entire life - until now. Whatever happens with this Gryffin guy and Avoca's plan - Bray intends to stay with the Hunters. It's where he belongs.

He gets himself a drink and opens the programming file on his unit. No harm doing a few final checks on the data. He can't help but smile to himself as he checks through his work. He's looking forward to seeing what kind of chaos he can bring to the Foundation and their plans.

If you enjoyed Mania, please leave a review and tell somebody about the book. Reviews and shares are always welcome.

Thanks for your support!

The adventure continues in

CRONUS

Nomad Series Book 6
Due 2022

Read on for an excerpt

1

Roman walks down the steps leading from the side of Infinity and looks around the base. He was only gone two days, but it felt like a lifetime. If someone had told him he'd ever be happy as a rebel commander in the Outer Sector, he would have thought them crazy. Yet, here he is. Up against the Foundation but also truly happy for the first time in his life. Well, the first time since Maggie, his first love left him and had his son in secret. A son who is occupying many of his thoughts recently.

His second in command, Tanner, a fresh-faced officer who was finding life in the Outer Sector as easy to adjust to as Roman had, stops at his left shoulder and hands him the report from their latest mission. 'Debrief now, sir?'

Roman takes the report and tucks it under his arm. 'Ten minutes. I want to see how he is first.'

He turns away and makes his way through the hustle and bustle of the hangar. *Ares*, with her unusual metal sails, sits to the left, her cargo ramp open as personnel move supplies around her hold. The menacing purple griffin glares over at him as he passes the back of the ship. *Nemesis* and *Epsilon*, along with one of the Rogue ships, *Dannan*, take up the rest of the bays. The rest of the Nomad, Hunter and Rogue ships are on patrol or ferrying colonists to safety.

Roman nods at any personnel he passes on his way into the belly of the facility. He finally reaches the heavy metal door and places his palm on the security pad. The door slides back and he steps into the holding cells. Four out of the five cells are empty. The occupant of the first cell is someone he's become somewhat close to over the last few weeks.

From the first moment over a year ago when he learnt he had a thirty-five-year-old son, things had spiralled out of control for him. Too many things had come to light, and to remain as level headed as possible, he pushed some of those revelations to the back of his mind. Dealing with the fact he had a grown son, who had been kidnapped as a ten-year-old by his best friend, Callum, was too much to handle at the time. His friend's jealousy of Roman's relationship with Maggie had put their son in danger. Crazed with jealousy, Callum had targeted Gryffin and spent years modifying him, altering the boy into a highly volatile cyborg. Unsurprisingly, Gryffin didn't want anything to do with his Foundation father and, at the time, Roman had accepted his decision.

But something changed over the last few weeks. He has a son. It's that simple. Finding out about their relationship was a surprise to both Roman and Gryffin, but it didn't change the truth of it. He has a son, and even if it takes him the rest of his life, he will try to get through to him.

Thankfully, it didn't take quite that long. Gryffin seems to be warming to him. It is far from a typical father/son relationship, but the Nomad leader is at least acknowledging him. It's a small but welcome start. Unfortunately, unless a miracle happens, they may not get the time they need to develop anything more.

His son is dying. Piece by piece, the modifications his twisted friend made are failing, taking more of Gryffin with them each time.

Roman settles into the chair in front of the cell and dismisses the Nomad standing guard. He quietly leaves the room, closing the door behind him. Roman leans forward and rests his arms on his legs. From what he can see, Gryffin's condition has worsened in the last two days.

He seems to be asleep, but his rest is far from soothing. There's no comparison between the intimidating man he met a year ago and what's facing him in the cell. Apart from the damage the implants are causing to his body, they've also had to remove his prosthetic arm. After nearly electrocuting Milla it was decided for his safety - and theirs - to take it off. Even without his lower arm, small sparks of electricity still race across the surface of his exposed stump.

His pale face is damp with sweat, the few days of stubble helping to mask his sunken cheeks. He had cut his hair, losing the long locks that hid his facial implant and scars from view. The short, dark spikes helped keep him cool through his frequent raging fevers, but even they are soaked in sweat. Without his long hair, there's nothing to hide the large scars on his face.

The anger still burns in Roman's gut when he sees them. The more serious of the two, the one that stretches from over his right eye, across the bridge of his nose to his left cheek was done with a broken bottle while he was in Tyrat prison. At least that's what Desyl told him. Gryffin never spoke about the myriad of scars on his body. Something that Roman can't help but be somewhat grateful for. Damn knows he's struggling with the little he knows about the torture his son has endured over the course of his life.

Gryffin mumbles in his sleep and thrashes in the bed. The black t-shirt rids up, exposing much too visible ribs. The 'W' shaped implant embedded in his skin seems to have sunken into his body creating a hollow that gives him a skeletal appearance. Not training or eating much has withered the once strong body. The rare times he's been interested in eating usually ends with the food making a reappearance. Milla was reduced to giving him high doses of nutrients to keep him going. Not being able to restock *Infinity* or *Epsilon* with Foundation grade supplies leaves her trying to utilise what they have left on board with the meagre and primitive offerings of the Outer Sector.

The metal brace supporting his right leg rattles against the bars as he moves on the small cot. It's his damn leg that's giving them the most sleepless nights. For reasons he will never comprehend, Roman's dear psychotic friend decided to add cybernetics and metalwork to Gryffin leg. He had left the lower leg as it was, choosing only to replace the outer layers of his upper limb with metal. Apart from leaving him with a near useless, excruciatingly painful leg, the living tissue imprisoned under the metal was so riddled with infection it was putting a huge strain on his system - both organic and artificial. Nothing they try makes it any better. The last discussion mentioned amputation. It is something Gryffin is dead against, but it is getting to the stage where he loses his leg or his life.

His other implants aren't faring any better. His robotic eye shut down before Roman left on this trip a few days ago and the other is less than reliable. He's also battling a brutal headache and nothing Milla does offers any relief,

Unable to watch Gryffin struggle with sleep, Roman

pushes to his feet and paces the small room. He's actually surprised Terra isn't here, keeping Gryffin company. While he hopes she's taking time out for herself, he knows she's probably under a console on *Ares*.

She's another person occupying his thoughts. Her feelings for Gryffin are plain as day - which in itself is troublesome. She's in love with him in spite of everything he's said and done to try to convince her otherwise. Roman knows she's going to get hurt. Whether thanks to his brutal childhood or something the implants did to him, Gryffin struggles with emotions. There is no question Gryffin cares about her, but Roman doubts it goes beyond that, or if it does, whether Gryffin comprehends what the feelings mean. It's not his fault, it's just how things are with him.

'How'd it go?'

Roman stops pacing and looks over at Gryffin. The Nomad is propped up on his remaining arm, squinting at him through unfocused eyes. 'I didn't realise you were awake.'

Gryffin uses the bars to pull himself up and manoeuvres himself into the corner. He collapses back between the wall and bars looking exhausted by the effort. 'How'd it go?' he repeats.

Roman sits down. 'Surprisingly well. The leaders of the colonies are going to continue working with us. Admittedly, at the initial meeting having the Nomad involved didn't fill them with confidence, but they came around.' Gryffin looks away and Roman knows he blames himself for destroying the relationships he spent so long forging.' Hey, this isn't your fault.'

'I was the one holding the gun. I attacked Ultar. I betrayed the colonies.'

'That gun was put in your hand by the Foundation. When they sent you to destroy Ultar, it was as much a tactical decision as it was a plain old attack. Everyone heard about it. They know it wasn't your fault. They know the Foundation programmed you-'

'Doesn't make a damn bit of difference and you know that. Might be best if I back out. Leave it to you and Desyl or Chayse.'

Roman shakes his head. 'Give it time. So far the leaders seem to be happy with me taking charge. They know the Nomad are still involved, but they'd prefer if it was behind the scenes for now.'

'You good to do that?'

Roman makes a face. 'With you stuck in there and Aleena dealing with the colonists here, I don't have much of a choice. I'm not built for the political life but needs must. You just need to give them time, Gryffin. So, how are you feeling?'

Gryffin smirks, 'Peachy.'

Roman laughs. 'Sounds like you've been spending too much time with Milla.'

'She suggested I try a response other than fine.'

'Can't say it suits you.'

Gryffin closes his eye and rests his head against the wall. 'Think I'll stick with fine.'

'Have you been able to eat anything?'

He shakes his head. 'Terra's taking it personally. Like I have a problem with her cooking.'

'Please say she's not cooking for you?'

'Don't tell her but I tasted better in Tyrat.'

'Burnt beyond all recognition?' Gryffin nods. 'Always happens when she cooks. Can't for the life of me figure out how she does it?'

'Yeah, well I wish she'd stop trying. Food is in short enough supply without her ruining what we have left.' He winces and looks over at him again. 'Anything from Earth?'

The question is innocent enough, but Roman can't help but feel there is a little brotherly concern at its core. His brother, Bray and the ex-inmate Garvan disappeared through the Port two weeks ago after hitching an unplanned ride to Earth on a Foundation vessel. Gryffin hooked to the nav system on *Ares* and brought himself to the brink of death by trying to catch up before the Foundation ship entered the Port. He wasn't successful and he's still paying for it.

To get his man back, Sayber had taken his ship *Perses* along with a Rogue ship to find them and bring them home. 'I've only just got back but I'm sure someone would have told me if there was.'

Gryffin nods and readjusts his leg on the bed. 'If Sayber and Bray don't make it back, they'll need to appoint a new leader and flagship. Quinn still here?'

'And not too happy about it. I'm getting the impression he'd much prefer to be on *Perses* then a grounded Hunter representative.'

'Can't blame him. The Nomad and Hunters on the surface haven't spent this long on solid ground before. We prefer to be on our ships.' He takes a deep breath and closes his eye again. Roman knows he would give anything to be at the helm of *Ares* again. 'You should talk to Quinn. Make sure he has a back-up plan just in case *Perses* doesn't make it back. Wouldn't want some other group taking them down while they're getting their shit together.'

'Should I be keeping an eye on your Nomad, Captain?'

Gryffin opens his eye and smirks slightly but doesn't reply. He readjusts his brace again and lets out a deep breath. 'I need you to do something.'

'Sure.'

Gryffin pushes himself further upright and looks at Roman. 'Talk to Terra. She's brushing my condition off like I've got a damn bullet wound. I've tried but she won't listen to anything I say.'

Roman nods. He had noticed her clear case of denial before he left but was hoping, with time, she'd allow the truth to sink in. 'I know Milla's tried a few times. You can't blame her for having a bit of hope. She's in love with you. Not giving up hope of a miracle goes hand-in-hand with that.'

'Hope is fine as long as she accepts it will probably go the other way. I'm not going to beat this, Roman.

'Gryffin-'

'I'm not. You know that. She needs to understand.

Milla thinks I have two weeks left at most. Terra needs to accept that.'

Roman leans forward and laces his fingers together. 'I'll talk to her but I'm not promising anything.'

Gryffin shuffles down the bed, bringing him closer to Roman. He takes a few deeps breaths, the exertion of moving from the top to the bottom of the bunk wiping him out. He leans his head against the bars and meets Roman's eyes. 'There's something else. I've said this to Terra but she wasn't taking it in. I don't want to die in a cell on Ultar.'

Roman swallows. He was expecting this conversation. That doesn't mean he's one bit ready for it. 'I've spoken to some of your crew about Nomad traditions. An honourable death is to go down fighting. As captain... being on your ship in your command chair is also acceptable. I'm taking it you want the latter. The first could be... well, an unfair fight.'

Gryffin laughs. 'Yeah. Takes the honour out of it when it's a slaughter. I'm not saying you let me out yet. Not much of a threat like this but not going to risk it. But when the time is... right, I want to be moved to *Ares*. Even if she stays in orbit. Just as long as it's not here... like this.'

'Of course.'

Gryffin nods and begins the task of moving back up the bed again. He lies down and closes his eye, quickly giving in to exhaustion. Roman slumps back in the chair and watches his son sleep. Never in his life has he felt so completely helpless.

In Foundation space, he'd be in with a chance, but trapped out here... He takes out his comms, but stops himself. Pressuring Milla and her team won't do a thing. They're spending every spare minute trying to find why Gryffin's programming stopped him from going through the Port. Until they find out why, they can't risk bringing him through. Even if that wasn't an issue, there's nothing to bring him across for. They're headlining the most wanted list. Earth is closed to them. Everyone he knows thinks he's dead. If anything, they'd be in a worse situation than they are here. At least here he's got a support system.

There's no point even considering any of that. He knows without a doubt Gryffin would rather die here than go to Earth. All he can do is make sure his death is an honourable one. If he wants to die in his command chair on *Ares*, then Roman will make sure that's exactly what happens. He just hopes Terra sees it that way.

ARES

NOMAD SERIES BOOK 1

(available as paperback, ebook and audio)

He wasn't expected to survive. No one else did, and for twenty years, he has managed to stay off their radar. Until now. Until her.

Gryffin was the sole survivor of The Foundation's experimental project to transform human children into hybrid cyborgs - half human, half machine. The program failed and he was sent on a one way trip into The Outer Sector where he was left for dead. He has survived for twenty years by suppressing his human emotions and embracing his machine side.

Officer Terra Rush believes in her duty to the Foundation. The Sector needs to be prepared for colonization, and nothing can stop her from doing her job...except him. When Gryffin saves her from an attack, Terra uncovers a terrible secret. The Foundation has been lying to her...and maybe they still are.

They have labelled Gryffin a killing machine, yet he acts more human than many of The Foundation's leaders. He has awakened intense feelings in Terra that throw her loyalties into question, and even though he pushes her away, she is determined to find out the truth about the cyborg program.

Gryffin refuses to be a mindless soldier, yet escaping The

Foundation's control and stopping the colonization of his home will require Terra's help. Can Gryffin overcome the machine inside and trust her? Or will getting in touch with his human emotions destroy him once and for all?

NEMESIS

NOMAD SERIES BOOK 2

(available as paperback, ebook and audio)

A part of her died when she lost him.

Commander Terra Rush has spent the last eight months mourning Gryffin, believing he died when his ship crashed. When he returns to her, broken and scarred from months of torture at the hands of the Foundation, it feels like a miracle - at first.

His unpredictable mechanical side, reawakened by the brutality he endured as a prisoner, threatens to destroy him. He's lost the trust of the colonists. Has he lost part of himself as well?

Her need to protect her ravaged heart puts distance between them when they need to depend on each other the most. If the colonists are to survive, they need Gryffin to reunite the Nomad and stand with them...and he needs Terra's help to do so. But time and tragedy have changed them both so much. Can they find their way back to each other before everything they know is destroyed?

PERSES

NOMAD SERIES BOOK 3

(available as paperback, ebook and audio)

On a mission to stop the Foundation from creating an army of cyborgs, wanted felon Brayden Sawyer is trapped far from his ship and crew in the last place he wants to be...Earth. With the Foundation hot on his heels, Bray must ask his family for refuge—a family who always preferred his brother Gryffin over him and kicked him out of their lives a decade ago.

When his family rejects him a second time, Bray wonders if saving Gryffin—and completing his mission—is worth it. All his life, he's been second best to his brother, a brother he never really knew. But turning his back on Gryffin is out of the question and he won 't let the Foundation do to others what they've already done to him and Gryffin.

Breaking into Foundation headquarters, Bray comes face to face with the horrible truth about his brother's cyborg enhancements as well as his own modifications. And that's not all...the Foundation is set to destroy a planet of innocent people, using Gryffin as their number one weapon.

With time running out, Bray must finish what he started. Together with Garvan and his family, Bray must escape Earth with the necessary technology to save Gryffin and stop the Foundation's evil plans. But can one man stand against the all-powerful and tyrannical Foundation? If Bray can save Gryffin, he may just have a fighting chance.

CHAOS

NOMAD SERIES BOOK 4

(available as paperback, ebook and audio)

Twenty-five years ago, two futures were changed.

Before becoming a Nomad and a Hunter, brothers Daegan and Brayden Sawyer were like everybody else on Foundation Earth. Then Daegan leaves for a school trip, a decision that would lead them to travel very different paths.

With his older sibling declared dead, Brayden's grief causes him to spiral out of control. After being banished by his family, he becomes even more self-destructive. When he's arrested and given a death sentence on the infamous Tyrat Prison, he realizes how far he's fallen.

However, Daegan is alive, though he may wish otherwise after discovering he's the latest recruit for the cyborg project. Years later, he finds salvation on the battleship, *Ares*. With their help, he becomes Gryffin and carves a formidable reputation for himself.

Chaos follows them as they fight their own demons and strive to find who they were always meant to be.